# THE COLLAPSE: TIME BOMB

## PENELOPE WRIGHT

Cover design by Nicole Conway

*For my husband, Travis Wright*

# PART I
# APRIL 19, 2006

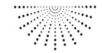

"She's going down the alley!"

I don't spare time for a look over my shoulder. These cops aren't on foot like last time. I'm dealing with bike cops, and I won't stay ahead of them much longer.

I thought it was a good plan, going to the methadone clinic first. Clearly, I'd been wrong. When I showed up at Seattle Needle Exchange, it was like they'd been waiting for me. Maybe they had been. This wasn't the first time we'd hit them. And it wouldn't be the last.

I tug on the knot that holds my shield sack to my body. It's tight and the bag's contents are secure. I try to push an extra burst of energy out of my legs. It's no use. I'll never make it to Columbia Tower before they catch me. My eyes dart around frantically and fall on Safeco Tower. It's farther downhill than Columbia, so I'll have to climb more flights of stairs before it's safe to plunge. But that's fine by me. Bike cops will have to dismount to follow me. Nobody from 2006 is going to catch up to me on stairs.

I dash into the lobby of Safeco. It's seven o'clock at night, but there's still a bunch of people around. I know this place almost as well as my own tower, though the lower floors aren't accessible where I'm from. I know exactly how to access the stairs from the ground floor, and I burst through the door and gallop up two steps at a time. A cop is right behind me, the door doesn't even close all the way before he's throwing his body against it, but I'm already on the second floor.

I have to get to the twentieth floor before I plunge. Safeco's only flooded up to the fifteenth floor, but if there's a storm, waves can send detritus as high as the nineteenth. I don't want to go home to the present, only to be knocked out by a rogue wave of junk. I hear the cops down below, out of breath, unable to keep up with me. I pull way ahead.

I allow myself a small smile when I reach the landing marked 18. The smile is wiped completely off my face when a stairwell door two stories above me smacks open with a hollow boom. "Hold it right there. You're under arrest," a man's voice shouts from above. Dammit! He must have taken an elevator to get ahead of me. I always forget about those.

Under arrest? Oh no I'm not. I can't let them take me to the King County juvenile detention center. Dad flew me over it once in a helicopter. It's way too far from the Towers. Even if I could somehow swim the debris filled waters between juvie and Columbia Tower, the radiation would fry me.

I whip my helmet out of my vest pocket and Velcro it all the way around my jacket collar. I ratchet the two locks on either side of my collarbone. The guy above me stands on the landing of the nineteenth floor. "What the hell are you doing?" he asks in bewilderment.

I push the extra-long sleeves of my jacket up to my elbows. I unzip my left vest pocket and peel away the second skin to reveal my port-a-cath.

The cop takes slow, cat-like steps down the stairs, his hands held cautiously out in front of him. "Just take it easy," he says. From below me, I can hear lumbering steps and the heavy panting of his partner.

I unzip my right pocket and pull out my hypodermic.

"Nobody move," the cop above me shouts. "The suspect has a weapon." His hand flies to his gun hip.

I flick the cap off the hypodermic needle. I don't have time for a proper countdown. *Plunge.* I thrust the needle into my port-a-cath and depress it. *Withdraw.* I slide it out. *Drop.* I open my hand and the spent hypodermic falls to the floor.

The officer throws himself at me, knocking me to the ground.

*Slap.* I flip the second skin back over my exposed port-a-cath, covering it up. *Zip.* I barely manage to zip the flap on my vest before the cop has wrestled my arms behind my back. He can't seem to find my wrists under the extra-long sleeves of my jacket.

It would be better if the cop wasn't here to witness this, but it's not the end of the world.

Everybody knows that's not for another thirteen years.

Spots bloom in front of my eyes and grow big enough to burst into a shower of black glitter, and I slip into the void.

# CHAPTER ONE

March 14, 2074

I emerge face down on the eighteenth-floor landing in Safeco Tower with my hands behind my back. My head pounds, but I have to get to a comm. The lowest year-round habitable floor is two stories above me, on twenty. I stagger to my feet and trudge upward.

Droplets of water mist the viewing shield of my helmet and I look to my right. There's a gaping hole in the brick. I wonder how long that's been an issue. It's been at least three years since I've been in Safeco. It's only two blocks north and a block down-hill from where I live in Columbia, but I rarely leave my own tower. Even the important adults don't building-hop much.

The climb to the twentieth floor isn't difficult at all, just a couple of pieces of flotsam to avoid. A picker must have come through recently. That and the day seems fairly calm. That's a stroke of luck, especially in March.

I breathe a sigh of relief when I reach the twentieth story landing but wonder who I'll startle when I emerge from the stair-well. It doesn't matter which tower you're in, only a couple classes of people go anywhere near the flood line, and I am obviously neither a flotsam picker nor a building inspector.

I shove open the interior door, the same one the cop burst through a few minutes ago, back in 2006. Dandelions and nettles grow in vertical hydroponic rows. An attendant mists precious pure water along the stacks.

"Excuse me," I call out, grateful that I didn't barge into someone's living quarters.

The attendant is so startled, he nearly drops his mister, which would have been a disaster, but he fumbles with it for a second and gets it back under control.

"Who are you?" He clenches his fists, like he's ready to dash my brains in.

"My name is Rosarita," I say. "Rosarita Columbia." He stiffens and straightens up at my last name. "And I need to borrow your comm."

The gardener nods curtly and leads me to a box with a button pad. He looks away discreetly, like we do, as I punch in the number to Dad's private line.

My father picks up on the first beep. "Hello?"

"Dad!"

"Rosie!" He bellows loud enough to wilt the plants, and my stomach rumbles. Wilted dandelion leaves sound wonderful. Man, I'm hungry.

"Hey…" I rub my toe into the smooth floor. "I had a bit of an issue with, you know, what I was working on. I'm in Safeco Tower. Can you, uh, come and get me?"

Ten minutes later, I'm slumped in a chair in General Enrique Safeco's quarters on the fiftieth floor. My head is pounding, which is weird, because the return trip usually isn't hard on the brain. Sometimes I lose my helmet in the past and I don't have it for the return. It's never been an issue. This time I was wearing it and my head feels like it's going to cleave in two.

The comm on the desk emits a burst of static. "Rosie?"

"General Safeco?" I answer. It's not my dad's voice, and who else would know I'm here?

"Yes. I'm sorry I'm not there to greet you. I had an issue arise on forty-five." As the commander of this tower and one of Dad's top military leaders, I'm sure he feels a responsibility to be here, but I'm also sure he has more important things to worry about than a wayward teenage girl lounging in his living room. What was I supposed to say? *I almost got caught stealing Botox and syringes sixty-eight years ago, and unfortunately I ended up in your building instead of mine, my bad?*

"That's okay."

"Your father commed. He's on his way. Wait five minutes, then go upstairs to the decon chamber and prep for transport. It's the same layout as Columbia, you won't have a problem finding what you need. If I can, I'll come upstairs to see you off."

"Thank you, Sir, I appreciate the use of your building and your facilities," I say. I don't tell him that I won't need the plastic sheeting in his decon room; the suit I wear when I'm time traveling is more than enough to keep the radiation at bay. Maybe I should put the sheeting over my suit anyway, to disguise it. Safeco doesn't know about the time travel program. Only Dad and I do. I don't want to waste the sheeting, but I also don't want to raise unnecessary questions in Safeco's mind about what I'm wearing.

I grind my teeth, then snap my jaw wide open. I need those molars to stay healthy. I'll decide what to do about the sheeting when I get upstairs.

I curl back into the cushy chair, and my mind wanders for the next few minutes. Dad might be upset that he had to use aviation fuel to come get me from the wrong tower, but he'll be really happy about the chemicals and supplies I've brought back. Hopefully my haul from 2006 is enough to cancel out the unnecessary waste of fuel. Of course, if I'd planned better, I wouldn't have been chased in the first place. I close my eyes. My five minutes are up.

I rise to my feet and climb to the decon chamber. A strip of test tape flutters just outside the window. It's to gauge the burn level. I know that the numbers one through five are printed on that test tape, but the one, two and three have faded, and all I can read are the four and five.

Ugh, a four. It's better than a five, but still, a bad day to have Dad flying around out there in a helicopter. I guess I should be thankful I arrived in Safeco Tower rather than somewhere farther away or harder to get to, like the Washington Mutual Tower, or, god forbid, the Space Needle. The less time spent outdoors, the better.

I hear rotor blades chopping the air, and Dad's helicopter is suddenly there in front of me, six feet above the roof's surface. I'm not going to sheet up. I don't need to; it's a waste of the Safeco Tower supplies, and no one's here to see me in my weird silver time travel suit anyway. I pull my flexible helmet from under my arm, jam it over my head, and step out onto the roof.

The helicopter touches down, its nose facing me. I see the pilot and my father seated side by side. I raise my hands in the air a second before the third man bursts out the helicopter's side door; I know the procedure. He points his machine gun at me. I make sure he sees that there's nothing in my hands. Keeping the gun steady, he wiggles his head to the left and the right, giving me permission – and an order – to take off my helmet. Well, at least I had it on for thirty seconds. I lift it over my head in a smooth motion. A smile cracks Dad's face briefly before his expression returns to his typical stern public façade.

Dad's guard pats down my shield sack, which is strapped across my body. I'm sure he's feeling for weapons, but he doesn't peek inside. Dad's orders, I assume. I keep my eyes fixed on my father, these pat-downs are standard but they always creep me out.

Dad's eyes widen, and he looks past me. He lifts his hand in greeting, and a weird expression flits across his face that I can't quite name.

General Safeco must have come upstairs, like he said he would, to see me off. I don't turn though. I'm not allowed to move a muscle until Dad's guard says I can. The guard's eyes flick to my father, who gives him the okay sign. He shoulders his weapon and steps aside so I can pass by and enter the copter.

Before I do, though, I turn to look at General Safeco. He's one of the oldest members of our community, so he's always seemed ancient to me. It's been about five years since the last time he came to Columbia in person, but he looks even older than I expect him to, and that's saying something. He was a teenager during The Collapse; one of the few people alive who remembers it. He must be around seventy now, but he looks two hundred.

Before I even know what I'm doing, I wave at General Safeco. "See ya later!" I call.

His mouth drops open and he presses his hands against the Gila-shielded glass. I'm mortified. *See ya later?* Where on Earth had that come from? I bet no one's ever treated him so informally in his own tower, let alone David Columbia's daughter. Now Dad will probably have to send a formal, respectful apology. God, could I screw this day up even more? I fall heavily into my seat in the helicopter. I avert my eyes and stare at my folded hands, properly deferential now, but just a bit too late.

―――――――

It doesn't take long to debrief Dad once we get back to Columbia. I wasn't gone that many days, and I *did* return with everything on the list.

From the debrief, we move on to strategy. Traveling to the

2000s means Google is everywhere, so I have the ability to do good research. I spent a little time at the Seattle Public Library and I found an article about a needle exchange in Tacoma that was founded in 1988. Of course we've never hit it, because we haven't known about it until now. Dad hadn't specifically given me a research goal, but he's proud of my initiative.

We brainstorm a future hypo mission. Tacoma is close enough that we can copter there and back in our time, if we wanted to. Not that we ever do. No one's gone there in my lifetime. Tacoma is nothing more than the tops of a few deserted buildings poking out of the water. Anything useful there was harvested decades ago. But now that I've learned they have a late-eighties needle exchange, maybe we'll make the trip.

Dad steeples his fingers together and touches his lips thoughtfully. "We could land a copter on 1201 Pacific. Nice flat roof, built in 1970, flooded to the twentieth floor, top three floors accessible."

I nod. "I could begin the journey from a stairwell on the twenty-third, twenty-fourth, or twenty-fifth floor. I'm sure I could find one that's easy enough to clear of debris. We wouldn't need a travel chamber or anything, there's no risk of anyone seeing me dematerialize since Tacoma's uninhabited. I could return to Tacoma as well, assuming we can spare the aviation fuel."

Dad inhales sharply at the word 'assume,' which is one of his least favorites. Assumptions get people lost or dead, and I immediately regret choosing that word. "I'm sorry Dad. It seems like whenever I go to the past, I act like a zed for a while." I put my hands over my face. "I waved at General Safeco and said 'see ya later' before I got in the helicopter," I mumble miserably.

Dad snorts and relief surges through me. I part my fingers and peer at Dad with a tiny smile. "He must have felt like a teenager," Dad chuckles. "I'll send an apology for your breach of protocol, but between you and me, I think it's funny, and I *am* the president."

The zeds I navigate around when I'm in the past would probably think the way we treat each other is crazy here in 2074, but when you live the way we do, with so little space and such limited resources, you must have order, and order demands formality. "Thanks, Dad."

"Let's wrap up for now. You brought back enough hypodermics to last us six months, probably longer. I'll see where we're at with av-fuel, and I'll let you know if we need you for a Tacoma mission. You did good work, Rosie."

I glow with pride. Dad loves me, but he's really stingy with compliments. These might need to last me a while.

"Head to your quarters." Dad pats me on the back. "Comm your letter-mate, get caught up on the last few days' lessons. Say 'hello' to Sarah."

My shoulders sag a fraction. If Dad notices, he doesn't say anything about it, he just gives me a couple more commands. "Listen to a game. Relax."

"With Sarah?" My face screws up. Spending time with her is the opposite of relaxing.

"If you'd like, but you're free to make your own choice. Perhaps your letter-mate. What's her name again?"

"Ellen."

"Ah yes, I remember. One of the Banks, is that correct?"

"Yes, sir."

"She's lucky to have you."

I feel lucky to have her too, but as a resident of one of the difficult-to-access Banking towers, Ellen was pretty far down the list to get a replacement letter-mate after her original letter-mate, Enid, died when they were seven. Failure to thrive. Ellen flew solo for four years. I was eleven when I lost Rachel. That's the way it is in the towers. Some people, like Enid, die. But far more, like Rachel, are simply lost, and we never know what happened.

I didn't have to wait for a replacement letter-mate like Ellen did; Dad intervened and paired us up himself. We didn't have to go through official channels or observe a waiting period. There're twenty-five of us left from our original litter cycle of forty-two children. It was a smaller than normal year for our litter cycle. The biggest one we've ever had was three hundred and sixteen babies.

Every year, the commanders of each tower perform a census. Food production, water stores, and other resources are counted and forecasted, and after blending those figures together, the tower commanders decide how many new children to incubate.

Most women lost the ability to have children within a few years after The Collapse, so they tested everyone and harvested the few remaining healthy ovaries, then stored the eggs cryogenically. A new litter cycle starts every year on April nineteenth, the anniversary date of The Collapse. Any man can donate his DNA to the gene pool, but with only a few biological mother eggs to choose from, most of us look a lot alike, and nobody knows the actual parentage of any of the zygotes.

A year later, the infants are harvested. Some are given to adults to raise, family-style, but most live on children's floors in one tower or another until they're six years old. That's when their skills are assessed and they're sent to a tower that's deemed most representative of their potential. The banking towers aren't good. But it's better than being a picker, living on a barge with no assigned tower, wading the half-flooded floors and sorting through the junk and debris that storms continually send our way. Traveling from building to building, never allowed past the second-lowest floor. I shudder at the thought.

I leave Dad's office and walk a few short hallways to my quarters. Our rooms are on the seventy-fifth floor of Columbia Tower. Dad's not only the commander of the most important building in the United Towers, he's also the president of our whole society. At fifty-four years old, he's the youngest living survivor of The Collapse. Most of us were born in the aftermath. Dad's mother, Rosarita Columbia, founded our world, ensuring the survival of humanity post-Collapse, and she taught Dad everything she knew. It's kind of hard to top that as far as leadership experience goes.

I walk through our quarters, my feet making scant noise on the thin, sixty-year-old industrial-grade carpet. "Sarah, I'm home," I call out.

I wait two seconds. No response. I look at our radio frequency ID floor plan. Sarah's dot is in her and Dad's room, but it's not moving. Sarah wears her chip in a bracelet. *She's probably asleep*, my brain whispers quickly. *Waking her would be rude.* I scurry to my room, delighted that I don't have to deal with my stepmom for the time being. At least I can honestly say I tried. Just, you know, not hard at all. I pull my own RFID necklace over my head. I never, *ever* wear it on a mission, but I always put it on as soon as I'm back in tower.

I walk to my comm and punch in Ellen's number. The comm emits a dull tone, and a couple seconds later, she picks up.

"Hello?" Her voice is crackly and distorted on the comm.

"Ellen, it's me!"

"Rosie?" Even with the static on the comm, I can hear the smile in her voice.

"Yes!"

"Where have you been?"

This is a first for me. One of the weirdest things about time travel is that no one ever seems to know that I've been gone. Sometimes I have to come up with excuses for why I don't remember things that supposedly happened in the last couple days, but no one has ever asked me where *I've* been. Dad says that in a few years, he plans to have me travel back and fill in all the gaps in time that I've missed in my own present. He says that just by saying his plan out loud, and meaning it, it's probably already come true in some dimension somewhere, which is why no one questions my absences. Because they truly don't even realize I'm gone because I've already made the lost time up. But I know that by doing that, somewhere in the future, I'll have other big gaps of time where I'm not around. It's like a constant game of leapfrog that I can never win. I try not to think about it too much because it drives me kind of crazy.

But that's why Ellen's question throws me for a loop. Dad and the technicians who help me prepare for travel are the only people who have ever realized I've been gone before, and they'd certainly never ask me probing questions about where I was the whole time. I should have planned for this contingency, though, and I'm irritated that I'm not better prepared. "Oh, um, I was in the infirmary." I'd spent two nights in the past, so that was how much time elapsed here. It seemed like a safe bet. "Doc wanted me there for observation for a couple of days."

"That makes sense," Ellen replies.

I'm not sure why it makes sense to her – I pulled it out of thin air with no explanation – but Ellen usually accepts my words at face value. I appreciate that about her.

Since she already seems to know I've been absent, I might as well ask her some questions so I can be the one in control of the conversation. "What's been going on in lessons?" I ask.

"We had another no-net climb. You'll probably have to make it up."

"Oh, man. How did everybody do?"

"Pretty good except for me. I almost bit it right at the end. I was a hundred feet up and the concrete gave away right between my toes. I was hanging on by my left hand and just flailing around with my right."

"Oh my God."

"I know. I'm all crazy, thinking 'this is it, I'm gonna die,' and the whole class is screaming, and right then my eyes fall on Boris's viewing window, and he's just absolutely thrilled, you know? He can't wipe the smile off his face, 'cause he's sure there's about to be an opening."

We lost Boris's letter-mate, Brian, nine months ago. Boris has been alone ever since.

"I would never be letter-mates with Boris," I say staunchly. "I'd fly solo."

"Well, you don't have to this time because that look of joy on his face pissed me off. I faced my fear, I let it wash over me, and when it was gone, I prevailed. I kicked a chunk of concrete out of the climbing structure and made myself a new toehold. Then I reached up a little higher and felt a knob. A real knob! Right there, five inches above my head. After that, I got myself up no problem."

"A knob! They hardly ever have those in no-net climbs."

"I know. I got really lucky."

"Or somebody in charge shot one out because they wanted you to live."

"Yeah, unlikely," Ellen says.

She's right, so I don't argue. My silence must go on a little too long, because she changes the subject.

"Wanna listen to a game together?" she asks.

"Sure." I reach over to my radio console. I twist the dial to turn it on and adjust the volume. We have one radio broadcast in the United Towers. Every once in a while, my dad or another top official will get on and make a speech, but usually the station plays a nonstop loop of sporting events or news programs from the past. I have most of the broadcasts memorized. I like the football, baseball, and soccer games the best. I always close my eyes and try to imagine the players: healthy, athletic people pushing themselves to the brink and beyond, not because their lives depended on it, but because it was fun. Right now one of my favorite recordings is on, a preseason football game from 2018.

Ellen and I listen to the broadcast together over the comm. We recite the football commentary word for word; Ellen has it memorized too. *Ellen's voice is shrill when she gets excited*, I think involuntarily. *Piercing*, my brain corrects. Strident. Authoritative. I love Ellen. I really do. And I don't like words with negative connotations regarding that girl, especially not when they're coming from my own disloyal brain.

Loyalty. It's huge for me. Closely intertwined is trust. They're different things, but you can't really have one without the other. She'll never be Rachel, but I'd still die for Ellen. I don't know what will happen to her when our training is over. As my letter-mate, she might be able to come to Columbia, to live and work in my tower. We're only sixteen, so we still have another year of scoring before anything's decided for good.

"Hey, Rosie," she asks, "is your heart in this one?"

I shake my head. My mind isn't in the game and Ellen needs me. Because when you're in your last two years of training, the instructors are always watching. Everything. Even something as simple as reciting a football game could be graded; it could be the difference between being a welder living on the forty-sixth floor of the Third Ave tower – or disappearing onto a barge for the rest of your life to sort flotsam. As David Columbia's daughter, I don't have to worry much about stuff like that, and sometimes it slips my mind completely. Ellen doesn't have that luxury. "Sorry. I'm not trying to wreck things," I say.

I slip back into the recitation. *"Colby spins back, scrambling, Drew is wide open in the end zone. Colby rears back..."* The announcer gasps and his voice grows wild. We match him word for word. *"And the ball is batted out of his hands. Is that a fumble or an incomplete pass? Was there forward motion? They're going to send this one up to New York, and we'll take a quick break."*

"You probably shouldn't use the words 'wreck things' after what happened with that helicopter," Ellen drawls during the brief pause in the broadcast. "Might want to reconsider your phrasing for a few weeks. Or years. Your call."

My eyes dart around the room nervously for a second before I get myself under control and I'm glad Ellen can't see me. "Ha ha, yeah," I say.

The game starts up again, but neither of us is parroting along with it anymore.

"What kind of punishment did you get?" Ellen asks.

How am I supposed to answer that? I have no idea what she's talking about. I try something vague but safe. "They went pretty easy on me."

"They went easy on you? Seriously? If it had been me, I would've gotten thrown off the roof."

A lump travels painfully down my throat. Barely anyone gets thrown off the roof anymore. Sent to the barges, maybe, or banished to a useless building like Insignia, but executed? Our population is too fragile for us to intentionally kill each other very often. *Thrown off the roof?* What had I done?

I decide to play it off like she's kidding. "Dad joked about that too."

Ellen's silence lasts a little bit too long before she responds. "I bet you got off easier because you got hurt. Enjoy freedom now; your dad might rain hell on you once your legs heal."

I look down at my perfectly healthy legs. "Yeah, maybe," I say faintly.

"What's the food like in the Columbia infirmary?" Ellen asks.

I don't know since I haven't been there in months. This conversation has veered left and gone straight out the window. I shake my head, glad Ellen can't read my mind. Deflect attention. Raise another subject. "Better than the stuff Sarah makes."

"Sarah? Ugh. She's so pointless."

"Yeah. But she's got great skin and my dad seems to like her, so there you go."

"I can't believe he married someone from Insignia. All those citizens do is fight with each other and cause trouble."

"Yeah." I decide not to say anything about my stepmother, or how Dad only met her three days before he decided to spend the rest of his life with her. I know all these things, but I don't want anyone else who happens to be listening in on the comm to be privy to them.

"How much older is your dad than her?" Ellen asks.

"Twenty-six years."

"Gross."

I can't help but agree with that. "Yeah."

"I never pegged him as the trophy-wife type, but stranger things have happened."

*You could say that again.* I almost mutter it out loud, and for a second I'm scared I did. Talking to Ellen is almost like thinking things over in my own mind; we've become that close over the years since we were paired up. And I know she would never, ever betray me. But I'm still surprised at how reckless I'm feeling right now. I'm really rattled.

The regular alarm bing-bongs through my room, as if my dad knows I need an escape route out of this conversation. "Hey, my dad's home. Let's comm again later. I want to tell Dad about your climb and ask him if he knows anything about the knob."

"Copy that," Ellen replies. "Tell me if he does."

"Roger." I switch the comm off and I take a quick look at our RFID floor plan. Sarah's dot is still in their bedroom. Dad's in his planning room. I slip my feet in my shoes and hurry to catch him before the opportunity is lost.

I rush through the hall and scurry to his office. I tap on his wooden door. I know he can see my dot so I don't have to identify myself, but I call out softly anyway as I knock. "Dad?"

"Come in."

My feelings must be written all over my face because when I walk through the door, Dad stands, opens his arms, and enfolds me in a hug. "Rosarita, Rosarita, my little refried bean," he croons, stroking my hair.

I blink rapidly. He hardly ever calls me that anymore. I turn my head to the side and nestle into his hug. The surge of emotion I feel is totally unexpected.

"What's the matter, Rosie? Did something happen? Is it Ellen?" He steps back and holds me by the shoulders, searching my face.

"Ellen's fine, but it does have something to do with her. Something she said. It's happened again, Dad. She says I got hurt. And...I think I might have stolen a helicopter."

Dad jerks his head, startled. He lets go of my shoulders and circles back around to the other side of his planning table and leans against it, palms down. "I don't know anything about a helicopter."

"Well, Ellen did. She told me I shouldn't talk about wrecking things after what happened with the helicopter, and she asked me what you did to punish me. I said not much, and she said you probably would once my legs healed."

"What did you say to her?"

"I deflected and then changed the subject to Sarah."

"Oh, great. Couldn't you think of any other topic?"

"I was on the spot, Dad."

"I'm sure you were very complimentary."

"Um...not so much. I criticized Sarah's cooking."

Dad sighs. "I suppose I should be delighted that you acted natural in the situation." He drums his fingers on the tabletop, thinking out loud. "I don't know anything about a helicopter. It could be that it's time travel related, and in the timeline that you and I are aware of, it hasn't happened yet. Make sure you note it in your journal."

That's it? I steal a helicopter – maybe – and injure myself – maybe – and all Dad can come up with is 'put it in your journal'? *Great.* I work so hard to leave an invisible footprint when I travel, but more and more, people are referring to stuff that I've supposedly done...that I have no memory of. I've got a growing list of timeline discrepancies, and I'm starting to worry that I've inadvertently caused a conundrum – a logical impossibility that is nevertheless true – which could destroy our whole world. But no pressure. I'll just write this latest piece of the puzzle down in my diary, and maybe I'll know what it means in forty years. Or maybe it'll be crystal clear after my next mission. Dad's advice is always the same: redirect the conversation and stick as close to the truth as possible so I don't have to keep track of a million made-up cover stories, then journal it afterward. I feel like I need more than that, but what do I expect from him? He doesn't know what do to with a conundrum. We've never had one before. That we know of. Maybe we're living one right now.

I roll my eyes, my head sags forward, and Dad misinterprets my thoughts.

"Did you say 'hello' to Sarah when you went to quarters, like I told you to?"

I keep my head down. "I said 'I'm home' and no one answered."

Dad is silent for so long, I finally look up. His lips are set in a thin line. He blows a long stream of air out of his nose. "Rosarita, it was just you and me for most of your life. I understand that my marriage is likely a difficult change for you, but you are an intelligent, capable person. Your inability to follow direction on this one boggles my mind. Return to quarters, locate your stepmother, and be cordial until I arrive. That is an order."

I grind my back teeth together involuntarily. "Yes, sir." I stand up and walk to the door, knowing I've been dismissed.

"Rosie?" Dad says softly.

His change in tone surprises me, and I turn at the door. "Sir?"

The expression on his face is one I almost never see. The word 'vulnerable' springs to mind, and I don't know if it's completely accurate, but it's the word my brain is supplying. "I know things are strange right now," he says, "and I don't have an explanation for all of it. But you need to know one thing. I'm the luckiest father in the history of the universe."

Tears spring into my eyes.

"I love you," he continues. "That is an immutable fact, and no slip in the space time continuum will ever change it. I need to make that very clear."

"Thank you, Daddy," I choke out.

Dad's face slides back into his usual gruff mask. "Now. Go be nice to Sarah."

This time when I say, 'Yes, sir,' I sound like I mean it.

# CHAPTER TWO

March 14, 2074

Sarah's RFID dot is still in their bedroom, so I tap very gently on her door. I need to wake her up and have a productive conversation with her, I promised Dad, but I don't want to startle her out of her nap and get off on the wrong foot.

I hear a muffled groan from behind the door, and a staticky pop, as if she's disconnecting the comm. "Come in."

The lock mechanism disengages with a click and I push the door open.

Sarah sits with her back to me at her dressing table. She's brushing her hair, and our eyes meet in the mirror. I don't want to look away first, but I also don't need to begin this interview with a staring contest. I'm here to be nice. I avert my glance. "I thought you were napping," I say.

She sets down the hairbrush. "And yet you disturbed me anyway." She swivels her chair around. "Why are you here?"

I shrug. "Dad told me to come."

"Ah, I see. Can't even be friendly without Daddy's say-so."

"No, it's not that," I say, holding up my hands reflexively in front of me but quickly dropping them to my sides in defeat. Because maybe it is that. But I try again anyway. "How are you doing today? May I sit and visit?"

Sarah rolls her eyes in the direction of her sitting area. "I've been meaning to have a word with you." She flicks her hand toward the chairs. "Go ahead and wait there while I get dressed."

Well, that doesn't sound promising. But I go ahead and seat myself where she tells me and she disappears into the recesses of her and Dad's chambers, where I assume she's taken over most of the bathroom and closet space.

No one seemed surprised when Dad came back with her after a trip to the Insignia towers, except maybe me. Dad had girlfriends here and there, but he'd never moved one into our quarters in Columbia and called her his wife. And everybody just acted like it was totally normal. Tower commanders sent gifts. Their wives – who were all twice her age – commed Sarah with advice and gossip, but Sarah was frosty and the calls petered out.

I tried too. Sarah's only thirteen years older than me, so we should have been able to find common ground. But I seem to irritate her more than anyone else. She's been here almost three months. I would have given her the boot after three days, but Dad doesn't seem sick of her. It's like he doesn't even notice how she acts toward other people.

After a few minutes, she glides back into the room and settles herself on the chair opposite me. I stare. I can't help myself. A few years after The Collapse, when most women stopped being able to have babies, they harvested the eggs of the few fertile women left and started the litter cycle. Most of us look a lot alike. Dark brown hair, light brown eyes. Back in the past, our look was called Mexican. Mexico was a country, I guess. Every once in a while, though, someone will pop out of a litter cycle looking like Sarah. Dad says it's called Nordic, but I've never come across a country called Nord in any of the stuff I've read about the past. I assume they must have had blonde hair and blue eyes and long arms and legs. And if Sarah's any indication, they were also spiteful and mean.

She's wearing a black wrap-around dress that shows off her legs. Her feet are stuffed into completely impractical silver stiletto heels that are a little too small for her. Her toes poke out past where the shoe ends, but they still look great on her.

"So, uh...how are you?" I ask lamely.

She crosses her legs and holds a hand in the air, palm out. "I didn't invite you in to chitchat. I'm not trying to be your friend, Rosie. I just have one thing to say to you. Keep your sticky fingers off my things. This is not a community property family. Just because I'm married to your father, that doesn't make my belongings yours."

I jerk back. "Excuse me?"

"You heard me." She twists her foot in a circle. "I had seven sanitary napkins at the end of my last period, and now I have five."

"And you're accusing me of taking them?"

"I don't think they spread their little wings and flew out of my toiletry kit."

I fold my arms across my chest defensively. "I've never had a period. Even if I had, though, I wouldn't take your stuff. I'm not a thief."

"Oh really?" Sarah raises one eyebrow, another thing that her face does perfectly. "That's not what I've overheard you and your father discussing. It seems to me you're always sneaking around with a bag of stolen goods and a pile of sins to confess. He's quite lenient with you. In any other tower, your behavior would have you thrown off the roof."

Has she seen me going into Dad's office with my shield sack? Does she know what I've really been doing? I can't feed her any information that's off-limits, but I also can't just let her statement lie there without responding. "You've been eavesdropping on me and my father?"

Sarah lowers her lashes and peers at me coyly, like she's 'got' me.

I lean forward. "In any other tower, spying on David Columbia's private conversations would have *you* thrown off the roof."

Sarah uncrosses her legs and balls her fists at her sides. "Ungrateful little thief."

I'm shouting now. "I didn't steal anything from you! You probably miscounted. Or you made it up, just to have a reason to talk about getting your period." I stand up. "Congratulations. I'm happy your uterus works. Next time you want to brag about it, just say so. You don't need to accuse me of a crime first to give you a reason."

She jabs her finger at me and shouts. "You took them. I know you did, and I demand you give them back."

A bark of unexpected laughter pops out of me. "If you honestly believe I took them and used them for myself and now you're asking for them back, I gotta say, that's super gross." I get up and walk toward the exit door. I don't need to put up with this.

"You're a thief and a liar!" she screeches at my back. "You took my sanitary napkins and you used my lip gloss too! I always line the wand up so that the top says Max and the bottom says Factor and when I went to put it on, it was twisted the wrong way. You're stealing from me and your father just lets you do whatever you want, but I won't stand for it, do you hear me?"

I turn around. "People on the twentieth floor can probably hear you, Sarah. You're embarrassing yourself and our family. Please stop."

Sarah stands up, teetering on her too-small shoes and glaring at me. "You're the embarrassment. Your father can barely show his face to the other commanders after that last stunt you pulled.

Where did you think you were you going to go, anyway? None of the other towers would have taken you, showing up in a stolen helicopter. You're an idiot. A selfish little brat who can't stand it when something doesn't go your way."

The helicopter? Not this again. Sarah misinterprets my expression of horror for shame, and she digs in deeper. "Your father can't get you out of every little bit of trouble you get yourself into. This time, the fact that you're David Columbia's daughter makes it even worse. People don't want a commander-in-chief who can't control his own child. They're worried about me, back in Insignia. They've heard whispers of dissent. If people mutiny...if there's a coup...you and your atrocious behavior will be a giant reason why."

*Mutiny* is the most dangerous word in Columbia Tower and I can't let her spit that out with no repercussions. I rush back over and reach up to shake my finger in her face. She's at least eight inches taller than me in her pointy shoes, but I'm not scared of her. "If people in Insignia mutiny," I say, "it won't be because of me. It'll be because no one in your home tower can control themselves. My dad was only there in the first place to quell a riot."

A smile coils across Sarah's face. "George and Gregor were fighting over me and it got out of hand. It's not my fault, but it did afford me an introduction to your father."

I gasp and my hand flies to my mouth. "Letter-mates? Fighting over you?" My lips curl back in revulsion. "And you seem so proud of yourself."

Sarah shrugs. "It doesn't matter to me. I wasn't interested in either of them. Your father came into our building and smashed the riot with brutal efficiency. It was quite attractive."

"And then you came home with him."

"He found me quite attractive too."

"Sarah, you are a horrid person. My father will figure that out soon enough, and you'll be right back to your crappy little tower. Maybe next time you cause a riot, no one will come to snuff it out because we don't need Insignia. They're just four hundred hungry mouths on a few worthless floors. You'll all be sent to the barges, and we'll leave your tower to rust."

"Your father will never send me away once I'm carrying his child."

I don't understand what she's saying. I'm his child. What is she talking about? "You're not that much bigger than me. I'd like to see you try," I snarl.

She laughs, a tinkling peal incongruous with her words. "I'm not talking about you, you idiot. I'm talking about getting pregnant and growing a baby that's David's blood. You're just some brown-haired runt he picked out of the litter by random chance. Your father deserves to have a child of his own, one he made himself."

She's out of her mind. "No one's had a baby in over fifty years," I say.

"It has to happen sometime," she trills. "Radiation levels are down. I've had four periods in a row. I'm the most beautiful, healthy woman in all the United Towers. Once I'm pregnant, your father will do anything I want."

"But we have rules, Sarah. Rules even my father has to obey. He's only allowed one child. And I might have come out of a litter cycle, but he loves me more than anything. He would never renounce me or cast me out."

"Your father is the president. He can do whatever he wants."

"Maybe he could, but he won't. He's a good leader. He doesn't bend or break the rules to benefit himself."

"Then I'll just wait until you come of age. That's only two years from now. At that point, whether you stay in this tower or not, you'll be an adult and David can have another child. A child of his own blood, who will grow into a leader like him and your grandmother before him. A child who looks just like him, who he'll love so much more. You'll fall out of favor. At best, you'll be a servant in my home."

I stare at her in shock. In the course of a few minutes, she's gone from accusing me of stealing her sanitary napkins and lip gloss to telling me she's going to extinguish my father's love for me. What a psycho. "You might have your period now, but if we get a solar flare on the wrong day, all the Gila screens in the world won't help you. You better hope that doesn't happen before I turn eighteen."

Lightning fast, Sarah's hand darts out and grasps a chunk of my hair. She pulls and twists until my neck is nearly backward and I'm staring up at her. "Don't threaten me, you little runt. I may be beautiful, but I'm still from Insignia. I know how to fight dirty."

If only my father could walk into this scene unannounced. But of course the regular alarm goes off any time someone from the family walks through the door, so when it peals in their sitting room, Sarah immediately releases me, straightens up, and adjusts her skirt. She whips out her lip gloss and reapplies it, then thrusts the wand back in and twists the cap shut methodically. She holds it out on display. "Max. Factor," she says, then cracks a fiendish smile, showing all her shiny, perfect teeth.

Dad walks into the room. "So nice to see the Columbia women bonding at last," he says, crossing to Sarah and extending his hand to her.

She rubs her palm surreptitiously against the couch and a clump of my dark brown hair mixes into the plush fibers. She takes his hand, and he bends to kiss it. Her eyes gleam with triumph, and I see myself out.

# CHAPTER THREE

March 21, 2074

Over the next week, I volunteer for a double shift every day. Eight hours of inspections, an hour off for a meal and a rest period, then another eight hours of inventory control. I'm not the fastest inspector in Columbia Tower, but I can diagnose a broken weld as well as the next person. I shine in inventory. I'm fast and efficient. I usually pull a few doubles a month. As David Columbia's daughter, it's my duty to set an example, but right now, I have to admit to myself that I'm really avoiding my quarters – and Sarah.

But roaming the tower is no salvation, either. I feel like everyone is giving me strange looks. Knowing, questioning, angry, fearful. The look on the face depends on the person, but everyone seems to have some special expression reserved just for me. I do my best to ignore them all. But like Dad says, I journal everything. Our time travel program is a closely-guarded secret, so it's not like I can just say, "Oh, those things you think I did, they haven't happened yet – you know how it goes." Because they don't. No one knows how it goes but me and Dad.

I can't help but stew, though, about everything. Sarah accuses me of stealing her stuff? She probably miscounted. That or an inventory crew analyzed her needs, decided she had too many, and reclaimed the resource. She may think being David Columbia's wife makes her immune to things like that, but it doesn't. Yeah, she gets more credits to spend on flotsam so she has cuter shoes and better clothes, but she doesn't get to stockpile resources. No one does.

But her accusation hits a raw spot. In a way she's right. I *am* a thief. But only because I have to be. And it's only in the past, with the zeds. Lifting their wallets so I can buy the items we need or breaking into their businesses to steal the things no amount of money can buy…. I tell myself it doesn't matter. They're all dead anyway. I try not to look at any of them or interact in any fashion. I keep to myself in the past. I go in, do the job, and get out. I'm good at it. In the past, I steal because I have to, to save the real people in the present. I might hate Sarah, but she's a living human being, and I would never steal from her.

I'm on the forty-third floor helping Dental inventory their fluoride tablets when Dad comms and orders me up to his office. I cross my fingers and hope for another mission. No one will miss me, and maybe when I get back, this helicopter thing will have blown over. Dad might even be sending me back to fill in the gaps in my timeline now.

At the seventieth floor stairwell, I have to pass through a layer of security to go any higher. They all know me, but I still have to type the new daily passcode into a keypad before I'm allowed to climb the last five flights of stairs.

I wonder again about that trip that I know is coming sometime in the future, when I'll come back to fill in the times that I was gone traveling. Will it happen soon? Or will Dad send me decades from now? I picture myself as a fifty-year-old, doddering around, completing my lessons and trying to pass myself off as myself. I'm snickering as I walk into Dad's office. It's the first time I've laughed in a week.

"Something funny?" he asks.

"Time travel humor. I just told myself a joke from the future. You'll get it someday."

Dad rolls his eyes. "Ha ha."

I sink into the high-backed chair that faces his desk and we just stare at each other for a minute. Usually when he calls me to his office, he's all business, but right now, he's just looking at me, like he's trying to memorize my face. I've had a question burning inside me all week, and I didn't plan to ask it – ever – but it just pops out almost like I have no control over it. "Do you ever wish you could have a child of your own?"

Dad's eyes widen and his nostrils flare. "A child of my own?"

"You know. One that's really yours."

Dad leans back in his chair, and he squints his eyes, studying me for several moments before he speaks. "I was there the day you were born. I lifted you out of the incubator myself. I kissed your toes. I named you after my mother. You are really mine."

I blink furiously, a strange prickling sensation in my eyes. My recent trip to the past might have left me with an unexpected reservoir of tears. We're not usually hydrated enough to cry, and I'm determined not to let these spill. "But what if you could have a baby that was biologically related to you? Wouldn't you want to do that?"

Dad folds his hands on top of his desk. "I can have a baby that's biologically mine any time I want."

"Dad. No one's had a baby the old way in forty years."

"I'm a time traveler, Rosie. The normal rules don't apply to me. I could travel back to any point in time that I desired, and have a baby 'the old way,' as you say. Once it was born, I could stick it in my shield sack, come home with it, and no one would be the wiser, except a zed from the past, who would probably miss it very much."

My mouth has dropped open while he's speaking.

"Have you noticed a younger brother or sister living in our quarters?"

I shake my head. "No."

He smiles. "That's because I have no desire for another child. No one could shine brighter in my heart than you, Rosie, and it would be a disservice to another child to even try."

A tear leaks out of the corner of my eye and I wipe it away. "It's just," I choke out, "some people think that a baby that's your own blood would be more special to you than a baby you adopt."

Dad purses his lips and breathes deeply through his nose. He glances rapidly around his office, like he's back in training and has to memorize the contents of the room. "You know how much I loved your grandmother," he says.

I nod. "You named me after her." Rosarita Columbia, my grandma, founded our world. She had the foresight to see The Collapse coming, and she prepared for it. Everyone who's alive now has her to thank for it. She was a great woman. A legend. But I never got to meet her. They lost her just before my litter cycle began. I'm sure that's why Dad decided to choose a baby, to fill the void in his heart that she left behind when she vanished.

Dad leans back in his chair, folds his arms across his chest, and contemplates the drop-ceiling tiles for a moment, but it doesn't take him long before he seems to come to some sort of decision. He straightens up in his chair and gazes at me levelly. "Grandma adopted me."

My eyes pop wide open. "What? Really?"

"Yes. She rescued me from The Collapse when I was two days old. I don't know who my biological mother was. Your grandmother raised me as her own, and that makes me her own. Just like you are my own. You don't have to have my blood type to be my child, any more than I needed Grandma's blood to be her son."

"Why didn't you ever tell me that before? Why keep it a secret?"

"Your grandmother said when the time was right to tell you, I'd know." Dad smiles again. "Like with so many other things, she was correct."

"I promise I won't tell anyone."

"Your grandmother raised me to lead the Towers when she was gone. I suspect she didn't want there to be any issue with succession when she died," Dad says. "And there wasn't. It was a peaceful transfer of power, and I've been in command for nearly seventeen years. Now that I've told you, it's no longer a secret. Tell whomever you want."

I sigh. "Nobody seems very interested in talking to me right now."

Dad waves his hand dismissively. "They'll get over it. Maybe a new mission will help them forget all about it."

I snap to attention. "I'm traveling? When?"

"Today." Dad pulls out a pad of paper. In 2074, we rarely use paper; it's a finite resource. We have no means to produce it, so all we have is what happened to be in the Towers on the day of the Collapse. In the early days, stupid people with no foresight would defy my grandmother's rules and burn anything papery for warmth. After several Towers burned like matchsticks, fire was completely outlawed, but by that time paper was already scarce.

I've brought back a few pads of paper from the past, and they're worth their weight in Vitamin D liquid gels. Dad always writes my travel plan down right before I leave. I know I'll be headed straight to the prep room from here.

"What's the objective?" I ask.

"A few different tasks. Important, obviously, but they shouldn't be difficult. You'll be going to 2007. We need tetanus boosters. As many as you can carry in your shield sack."

"What's my target amount?"

"Whatever you can get your hands on. I'd call a thousand or more success."

I nod. If Dad wants a thousand, I'll bring him double that.

Dad goes on. "The Seattle Muni Tower will only be a few years old. I need you to conceal a lockbox within an interior wall. You choose the location. You can tell me where you placed it when you return. Of course, it needs to be away from elevator shafts, and remember, twentieth floor or higher."

Seattle Muni. The tower right next door. Fifty-seven stories, office layout. It would have been a great place if it weren't for its stupid rounded roof that you couldn't land a helicopter on. It wasn't like the architects had designed it to survive the end of the world, so it wasn't their fault that it *had*, and that its dumb roof made it so impractical. Muni's proximity to Columbia was its saving grace. We had rappelling lines strung between our sixtieth floor and its fifty-fifth. We could zip people down quick – the lines were higher on our side – to make it easier for us to get there if we needed to. Anyone who needed to get from Muni to Columbia had to have our permission, and be winched up by someone on our side. Fifty-five years since The Collapse, it was unlikely anybody from another tower would try to invade us, but that hadn't been true in the beginning.

"Like I'd forget about the twentieth floor or the elevator shafts."

Dad squints his eyes. "Did you get a good look at General Enrique Safeco when you wound up in his tower after your last mission?"

I shake my head. I hadn't. I'd only taken my helmet off just before boarding my dad's helicopter, and then I'd only glanced back to wave at him and utter my appallingly inappropriate 'see ya.' He'd looked the same to me. Ancient. He's one of the few people alive who actually remembers The Collapse. He was a teenager when it happened, so he had to be like seventy-something now. He's old, important, and definitely not part of my social circle.

"Well, when you do, you might notice he's aged a bit. We believe his helmet shifted in transit on his last trip. He arrived in 2014 with no memory of who he was or why he was there. He spent years living on the streets and in various institutions before something sparked his memory and he used his chemicals to recall himself to our time."

My eyes popped wide open. "General Safeco's a time traveler?" I blink in surprise. It's incredibly weird to me that Dad had just casually outed General Safeco as a chrononaut. Until now, I'd thought Dad and I were the only ones.

Storing that thought away to examine later, I try to wrap my mind around what Dad just said about Safeco's trip. "Whoa. So if he spent years in the past, he's been gone from Safeco Tower for that long?"

"Yes."

"I had no idea."

"Of course you didn't. You know how it works. Only three people realized he was gone the entire time. Myself, and the two prep technicians who helped send him. If you'd been in the planning room with us when we outlined his trip, you would have known too."

"Did you send him back to whatever date he departed, to repeat the time here, so no one missed him?"

"I must have at some point in the future, though I don't remember doing it yet. The Safeco you know, the one you met in his tower, is from the future. He's here, making up those lost years now."

"Whoa."

"Yes. Safeco has relayed very little of the details to me; you know it's not safe to talk about things that might be, or anything that occurs in an alternate timeline." Dad cocks his head. "There's no manual for time travel. We're learning as we go. Maybe all I need to do is say I plan to send him to make up the time – and mean it – in order for it to be as true as it needs to be for our purposes."

I shake my head. "Well, he can't possibly have many more years left in him. How much time can he spend traveling and then redoing the years? Couldn't you could send someone back to find him in 2014 and activate his chemicals for him and get him back to...when did he leave in the first place?"

"2070. And no." Dad shakes his head. "We don't have the resources to attempt a rescue mission. I thought he was lost forever. When he returned, he was very much alive and fully coherent. If, say, I sent you back to intercept him and return him to 2070 in his addled condition, I doubt he could seamlessly take control of his tower again. We don't know what jogged his memory and snapped him out of his fugue state, but he's fine now so I have no desire to risk his mental or physical health with a rescue mission. The General knows the risks associated with time travel, and he's fine with it." Dad grins. "Besides, after a few years in the twenty-teens, he came back to us with a fantastic tan."

I laugh, a short bark. Dad's sense of humor is wicked, and it comes out when I'm least expecting it.

He rearranges his face back to its typical somber expression. "So yes, Rosie, to get back to the point at hand, you might forget about the twentieth-floor requirement, so I've written it down on your plan sheet. And we'll be double-checking the security of your helmet before you depart, that's for sure."

Dad's office door swings open, and we both jump in our chairs. Dad slides the paper pad off the surface of his desk and onto the floor, but Sarah's probably already seen it with her round, shiny eyes. She tightens the knot on her bathrobe and slips into the room.

"What are you doing here?" Dad fumes. "You know you're not to come in when I'm in a planning session."

Sarah glides across the room and kneels on the beige carpet next to him, tucking her feet under her butt and looking up at him. "It's not a planning session – it's just Rosie." She picks up the pad of paper and sets it on the top of the desk. Dad grits his teeth, snatches it off the tabletop and slams it into a desk drawer.

Two veins have popped out on Dad's forehead and it looks like he's trying not to scream at her. Since it's time travel related, he can't correct Sarah and explain what I'm actually doing here.

"I had to pass through security on seventy to get up here. Maybe you should put some guards outside your bedroom door, Dad, to keep unwanted people from coming down the hall," I say snarkily.

Dad and Sarah both ignore me.

She sticks out her lower lip petulantly. "I knocked."

"No, you didn't. We're not deaf," I snap.

Dad must be thinking the same thing, because he's not putting up with any of Sarah's nonsense today. He stands up and hauls her to her feet. She unties the knot on her bathrobe and wiggles it off her shoulders and lets it drop to the floor. She stands defiantly, clad in tall black boots and a red dress that barely skims the tops of her thighs. Not just any red dress. *My* red dress. The one I bought before my last mission, with the credits I'd saved for six months. The one I haven't even had a chance to wear yet.

"That's my dress," I whisper.

"Oh, please, Rosarita, this would never fit you." Sarah sneers. "I got it from a picker two days ago."

"You didn't get that from a picker, you got it from my closet. I spent six months of credits on that."

"My word, Rosie, six months of credits for a dress? That's a lie and it's absurd. David, you really need to teach your daughter the value of money."

"Watch your tone, Sarah," David warns, his voice tightly controlled.

On the wall to Dad's left, a computer screen blinks to life, one of the few in the towers that still functions. It displays a wall of bright red pixels, interrupted by one black word in foot-high capital letters. ACHTUNG.

The emergency signal.

"Frack! Now?" Dad loses his grip on his anger and slams his fist to his desktop. "I have to go." He pulls the pad of paper out of the drawer and rips off the top sheet, folding it hurriedly, then handing it to me along with a stubby pencil. "Your list," he says to me. "And one more thing. I need you to paint the west wall on the fortieth floor blue."

"The mural?" I ask, shocked.

"No, god no. Leave that as is." Now the look in Dad's eyes is haunted, and a bit wild. "I'm talking about the wall next to it. Now go. They're waiting for you on twenty-one."

Sarah, standing and twisting her toe into the carpet, glares malevolently at me. "David, I came in here for a reason," she says.

My dad interrupts her. "To start a fight? Because that's what happened."

I know I need to leave now to complete the mission, but I feel like I'm stuck and I want to scream. Sarah stole my dress. After accusing me of being a thief, she stole the one beautiful extravagance I'd ever allowed myself.

And then there was the whole issue of my time travel. This was not the way my mission should start, with hurried orders and a verbal shove out the door. Should I stay and get more instructions from Dad? No, he's already written them down. And if I stay here, I'll have to witness the rest of Dad and Sarah's fight, and – god forbid – a hurried make-up kiss before he dashes to the helipad. I shudder involuntarily at the thought. Dad notices. "Go, Rosie," he says gently. "I love you."

I drag my RFID chip necklace over my head and drop it on Dad's desk, then I spin on my heel and rush out of the office, but not before I'm speared by a look of pure hatred from Sarah.

"This room is off-limits," I hear Dad yell before I enter the stairwell and the door clangs shut behind me. Dad won't be following me. I'm going downstairs, to the lowest level we can safely occupy year-round, the twenty-first floor. Dad will be taking a helicopter to Smith Tower to pick up his Achtung. Not much of Smith Tower is above the water line. It has a pointy roof and you need a grappling hook and a zip line to get in. I've never been there.

I shake my head. Someplace else I've never been is 2007, but that's going to change as soon as I'm suited up, prepped, and ready. I have almost sixty flights of stairs between me and the travel center. I'd better get a move on.

# CHAPTER FOUR

March 21, 2074

Twenty minutes later, I'm on the lowest useable floor in our tower and I've put in the daily code as the first step in the clearance process. Beverly, the guard at the door, knows me well by now – this will be my seventh trip – but she still has to run my fingerprints.

I press them against her glass pad.

She squints at the readout and sighs. "Prints are too faint, as usual." She smears mineral oil all over my fingertips to get the images to show up cleanly enough to match a dozen points of comparison. She gives me a baby wipe to clean up with. I notice the package is getting low. I brought two packs of baby wipes back with me on my third trip. Maybe I should score some more this time.

Beverly's eyes flash back and forth, scanning the screen, then she sits back and nods to her partner, who's been holding me at gunpoint until my identity is confirmed. He shoulders the weapon and steps aside to let me pass.

I wonder if he or Beverly knows what's beyond this door. Probably not.

I walk into an innocuous-looking hallway, nod goodbye to the guards, and shut the door behind me. I walk to the end of the hallway, open the far door, and step into the travel prep room, where Lisa greets me.

Lisa has short brown hair like I do, and the lines around her eyes and mouth make me guess that she's probably close to my dad's age. I've never seen her anywhere else in the tower but this prep room, so she might be a bit older than I think she is. If she never leaves the center of the building, her radiation exposure is lower than everyone else's.

She's always been the person who preps me for travel. The outbound leg of time travel is way harder on your body than the return, so it takes longer to get ready when I'm leaving on a trip. When I've finished my work in the past, all I need to do is get to a safe spot and plunge, but traveling to the past requires more safeguards and special equipment. I can't just go in my regular clothes. I slip behind a privacy screen to undress, which is kind of silly, because when I'm ready, I step back into the room, wearing nothing and holding only the piece of paper with Dad's list.

I lift my arms over my head and try not to be self-conscious as Lisa slides the vest portion of my suit down over my torso. She pulls a baby wipe out of a pack – also running low – and scrubs my armpits. I waffle with indecision. Baby wipes were not on my list. If Dad wanted me to get baby wipes, he would have told me. Maybe we don't need them as bad as I think. We had an especially violent storm last week. Maybe the storm unearthed a whole case of them, flinging them against the side of the building, and then they sailed through a twentieth-story window. Maybe a flotsam picker found them and exchanged them for a bottle of iodine pills and a gallon of fresh water. Maybe I should quit overthinking it and stop trying to second-guess my dad.

"We're nearly out of baby wipes," Lisa says. "Picking any up this mission?"

Was she reading my mind? I don't think they can do that, but hey, time travel exists. I guess anything is possible.

"Dad didn't tell me to get any. But he was kind of rushed; he got an Achtung before we were finished talking. Do you think I should?"

Lisa stares at me levelly. "I think you should do exactly what your father instructed you to do and nothing else."

A very legit response from someone who knows how lucky she is to live in Columbia Tower.

Lisa helps me into my outer jacket. The suit I travel in is light and flexible here in 2074, but in the void of time it becomes unimaginably heavy. Time travel doesn't take long, thankfully, but once you're in the void, you can't breathe from the pressure and the weight of inorganic material. When I travel, I bring nothing but the clothing on my back, my mission list and a shield sack tucked into a zippered inside pocket, and the port-a-cath implant necessary to make time travel work in the first place. When I return to the present I can wear regular clothes if I've lost my travel suit, but the only stuff I can bring with me is whatever I can hold or fit into the shield sack. I bet General Safeco can carry a much bigger sack than me. He's probably never screwed up the way I did on my second trip. In the void of time, those sacks full of inorganic material feel like they weigh about sixteen million pounds. You have to strap the sack snug to your body before you plunge your return chemicals or you'll lose it. I forgot to do that. God only knows where the sack with thousands of water purification tablets ended up when I lost my grip on it. Probably stomped on by a dinosaur or hurled so far into the future they've been swallowed by the sun. What a wasted trip. Dad was so disappointed in me.

I haven't messed up like that since, but I still haven't earned the right to carry a larger bag. The stuff I bring back is important, though. Bottles of multivitamins. Toothpaste. Contact lenses. I stole about two hundred pairs in all different prescriptions from an optometrist on my fifth trip. That made a lot of people very happy. They think our scientists are making big strides in providing the things we need to survive and keep humanity going until the planet heals itself and we can settle it again. And ultimately, we are. I mean, sure, we can't make contact lenses ourselves, but we figured out how to travel back in time to get them, which is pretty impressive.

People in the other towers don't need to know that the vitamin D liquid gels they take once a week came from 1998. They can just be happy that they don't have rickets anymore.

Lisa holds my pants out for me and I slide a leg into the loose, slippery material. Lisa wears purple nitrile gloves. I've rarely seen her without a pair covering her hands. She probably sleeps with them on. A box of those might fit in my shield sack. My list is short this time, I checked it on the way downstairs, to see if there was anything on there that Dad hadn't mentioned verbally. I'm supposed to get ten packages of sanitary napkins – I'm sure I know who requested those – and a thousand tetanus boosters. I don't know how big those will be, or how to get them. I'll be able to Google it in 2007. I'll have to go to a library and use their computer, then I'll have to figure out if I need to steal them from somewhere or if I can pick someone's pocket and buy them with cash at a store. Between research and on-the-ground planning and execution, this trip could take a lot of time. I might spend days in the past, maybe even a week or two. Luckily, no matter how long it takes, even years apparently, no one will miss me while I'm gone. That seems to be a pretty solid rule.

Another rule we seem to have confirmed is that you can travel through time but not space, so you better pick your departure point carefully, because that's exactly where you're going to show up on the other end of your trip. That's why we do it on the lowest floor possible. If I pop into 1992 in the middle of, say, a policeman's convention, the fewer flights of stairs between me and street level, the better. If I had to go any further back in time than 1985, we'd have to do it from another location since the Columbia Tower wasn't built then. I picture myself materializing into thin air in 1970s Seattle. I'm two hundred feet off the ground and plummeting to my death, frantically trying to plunge my return chemicals into my port-a-cath in midair to get back to 2074. No thanks.

The final proven rule of time travel is that you can't interact with yourself. I helped provide evidence for that rule after the water purification tablet debacle. Dad sent me back to try to stop myself from losing that stupid shield sack. I went back a day before my return so I could have a talk with myself and stress the importance of double-checking the security of the knots on my tie-down straps. I remembered exactly where I'd been, which streets I'd walked down, which buildings I'd entered, and when. It should have been easy. But every time I got within about a mile of myself, it was like I ran into an invisible wall of gelatin. Gooey and sticky and impossible to move through. I ran at the invisible barrier multiple times, and once I must have busted about five feet into it before I lost my forward momentum. Then it felt like an unseen hand was shoving me backward, my feet sliding along the cracked sidewalk, scuffing the soles of my stolen shoes. A zed passing by complimented me on my 'groovy dance moves' and tossed a dollar at my feet.

Since I couldn't interact with myself, I tried circling around and getting ahead of me. I left notes and signs for myself, in places I knew I'd be, where I thought I should see them, but I don't know what happened. I guess it didn't work, because even now, four trips later, that shield sack full of water tablets is still gone, and I still feel the sting of letting my dad down.

I told my dad about the gelatin effect in great detail, and the inability to approach myself. He understood, and he was actually grateful for the information. Now when he mentions that particular rule of time travel he calls it "Rosie's Law." I wish he wouldn't. I know he doesn't mean anything by it, but every time I think of how that all went down, I'm ashamed of myself.

Lisa slips booties over my feet, because regular shoes would be way too heavy for me on the outbound trip. The booties aren't much good for walking or running in, so when I get back to 2007 I'll stuff them into one of the inside pockets of my vest and go barefoot until I can shoplift some better footwear. One of Dad's goals is to go far enough back in time to open a savings account at a bank and let something called compound interest make money for us, so we don't have to steal everything we need, but it's a low priority. Dad worked out the math. For it to be worthwhile we'd have to go back at least to the 1930s, and Dad said it would be hard to find a bank that hadn't gone out of business during that time because everyone was suffering from depression, or something. I don't know. Dad is a lot more interested in zed history than I am, maybe because he lived through The Collapse too, even though he doesn't remember it. He was the youngest survivor – an infant, only two days old when it happened. Still, maybe it gives him a connection to that time that I just don't have. I'm way more interested in getting my people the things they need to survive right now. The people in the past...their politics, their religions, their art...they're just zeds, and I don't have the bandwidth to care about them. I care about the living. I care about the people in The Towers. My people.

I shake my head. Lisa has asked me a question and I've been so lost in thought I have no idea what she said. "Huh?" I ask brilliantly.

She smiles and I can tell that she's trying really hard not to roll her eyes. I must be the spaciest chrononaut ever. I wonder if she prefers working with General Safeco or if she thinks I only have this job because I'm David Columbia's daughter. Well, if she does think that, she's probably right. I wouldn't be here if I lived in Third, or Muni, or Russell Investments, or any of the other towers. I earned my position through trust. Dad knows he can count on me, no matter what. I focus my attention one hundred percent on Lisa. "Would you like to peel your second skin now, or after your gloves are on?"

"Oh! Now, please." I think it's way easier to peel the covering away from my port-a-cath with my fingernails. Maybe General Safeco likes to do it with his gloves on. And what if there're other chrononauts. There could be. I don't know. This whole Safeco revelation has whirled into a sea of unanswered questions.

Lisa fluffs open my coat and unzips the access panel on the upper right quadrant of my vest. I flick at the second skin patch until it peels back a little. I grip the nub and pull it further to reveal the circular white port imbedded beneath my skin.

"I look forward to your missions," Lisa says conversationally. "I'm always given plenty of time to prep you, it feels so much safer than the last-minute trips they've been thrusting at me lately."

Wow. I guess there are other chrononauts. I'm not sure I should be hearing this kind of stuff. What is up with everyone lately? Lisa has always been nice, but she's never been anything but businesslike. First Dad casually outs Safeco as a time traveler and now Lisa's complaining about her job? "I thought this prep routine was a requirement," I say, trying to keep my voice neutral.

"No, just guidelines," Lisa replies. "Best practices, if you will." She blinks a couple of times and reaches into the plastic bin at her feet. "Gloves," she says.

I hold out my hands and she puts them on.

"Last step, helmet."

"Make it nice and tight," I say.

"You'd better believe it."

I wonder if Lisa was the one who helped General Safeco into his suit when he left four years ago. Well, if she did, she's the best person to suit me up now. She won't make that mistake twice, just like I'll never use anything but a bowline knot to secure my shield sack to my body again. Mistakes. If they don't kill you, they leave you a lot smarter than you were before.

I dip my head and Lisa gathers my hair into a stubby ponytail and slides a hairnet over it. She places the silver helmet gently over top. I straighten my neck and she secures the bottom of the helmet to the collar of my vest with Velcro, then engages the lock levers on either side of my collarbone, really cinching it down tight. This is the heaviest part of my travel suit, and I know from experience that the weight of it in the void can leave me with a crushing headache that sometimes lasts for hours when I come out on the other side.

Lisa threads a silk-crete cord through a loop on the exterior of my helmet and then ties the other end to my right wrist with a simple slipknot. This precaution isn't for the void, it's for the other end. I have to take my helmet off right away when I land – it's the one thing that will draw the most attention to me – but it's best if I can bring my helmet home with me when I return. I've lost a few helmets in the past, sometimes it's unavoidable, but the materials they use to make them are in short supply here in 2074.

I have a two-inch-wide, six-inch-long viewing window in my helmet, and I meet Lisa's eyes through it. She gives me a thumbs-up, and I give her one back. "Final check?" she says, raising her voice so I can hear her over the muffling effects of my helmet.

I lift my thumb a little higher to indicate *yes* to that question, then spread my arms and take a wide stance. Lisa walks around me in a full three-hundred-sixty-degree circuit. She inspects the armpits of my jacket, a spot notorious for extra wear and tear. She ends her circle in front of me, but when she speaks, it isn't to me. "She's ready to go."

A short man with a lot of hair on his forearms enters the room. I've worked with him before, every time I've traveled, but I don't know his name. He never talks. I suspect he's one of the mutes, but I don't know for sure – he's never opened his mouth in front of me. He gives me my chemicals. One hypodermic zipped into my vest pocket on the left side, directly opposite my open port-a-cath. The other hypodermic is placed in my gloved hand. This one is for now. The one in my vest is for the return. They both work the same way. When the time comes, I'll insert the hypodermic into my port-a-cath and inject the time travel serum directly into one of the large central veins in my chest. It takes about two seconds to start working, so I've got to be quick. *Plunge, withdraw, drop, slap, zip.* I chant those five words in my head as the hairy-armed guy swings open the blast door. Lisa has already left the room, slipping out and settling herself at a desk behind a Gila-shielded window in a little room just opposite the travel chamber door. The hairy guy gives me a thumbs-up, and I nod and mouth "thank you." I don't speak once my helmet's on. I can't risk fogging up the little window.

I step over the threshold and he swings the door shut behind me with a clang that shakes the floor. I walk to the center of the small room and turn around so that I'm facing the blast door. There's a porthole in it, and beyond that, Lisa sits in her small control center. The travel room is completely empty – no carpet, no furniture, not even a comm. I'll keep visual contact with Lisa and she'll count me down using hand signals. She's a little warbly since I'm looking at her through the tiny view window of my helmet, then through an eighteen-inch-wide porthole, across the prep room, and through her Gila-lined window, but my eyes are plenty sharp enough to count the fingers on her hands as she marks me down.

*Five.* I flex my left hand and make sure my arm is hanging loosely at my side.

*Four.* I crack my neck quickly, right side, then left.

*Three.* I bend my right arm at the elbow, fingers curled around the hypodermic needle.

*Two.* I swivel my wrist ninety degrees.

*One.* I slide the tip of the hypodermic needle into the port-a-cath, my thumb flicking out from my fist and settling on the plunger.

Lisa cocks her head. *Go now!* My brain screams at me. *Do it!* But Lisa still has one finger in the air while she speaks rapidly to someone I can't see. My thumb trembles on the plunger.

Suddenly, Lisa spreads both hands wide and smacks her control room window three times. Her mouth moves in the wide, exaggerated motions of someone yelling at the top of their lungs. I don't know what she's saying. What happened? What's wrong? Is she telling me to stop, or is she saying to get into the void as fast as I can? I'm torn with indecision, and Lisa is still just standing in the room, pounding on the window and yelling.

I've been so focused on her, I nearly plunge my hypodermic from shock when a big hairy arm slaps a sign across the porthole on the blast door. "ABORT."

I yank the tip of the needle out of my port-a-cath. My knees go rubbery and I tremble all over. *Keep it together*, I chant internally as the wheel on the blast door spins and the hairy-armed guy jerks it open.

If he can tell that my body is as loose as a wilted leaf, he doesn't say anything. The hypodermic needle rolls a little too freely out of my hand and into his collection tub, like I'm dropping it instead of giving it to him intentionally, and he doesn't call me out on it. Whether he's one of the mutes or not, whatever his reason is for staying silent, I appreciate his discretion. He exits through the same door he entered before, taking the hypodermic needle with him. I'm breathing deep, controlled breaths. I'm not going to let Lisa see how rattled I am when she unlatches my helmet and takes it off.

"You okay in there, Rosie?" she asks, lifting the helmet from my shoulders. She hands it to me, and I fold it and slide it in the side pocket of my jacket in a smooth, practiced movement, just like I would have if I'd completed the travel and was out on the other side.

"I'm fine," I say, and I surprise myself with how calm my voice sounds. Like I just finished something mildly exciting, like a difficulty three climb, or a live ammunition riot drill. My voice definitely didn't sound like someone who got yanked out of a time travel mission one second before she was supposed to plunge into the void. "What happened? Is everything okay?"

"Yes," Lisa says. "Well, no. I mean, I don't know."

"What's going on?"

"I got an urgent comm on the private line, the one that comes directly from your family's floor. Your mission has been aborted. You're to proceed immediately to the roof, where you'll meet your father."

"My dad?" I exclaim. "He's back already?"

"Actually, I'm unclear on that." Lisa stamps her foot; she's obviously upset with herself. "You're either meeting him or being taken to him. I'm sorry. I can't confirm which." She lowers her eyes. "I was a bit flustered."

She's taking a big risk telling me that. I know I'm not supposed to touch anything with my travel suit on, but I put my gloved hand on Lisa's upper arm sympathetically. "So was I."

Lisa gives me a tight-lipped smile and a look of gratitude. "You'd better get up there as quick as you can."

I don't even take the time to rip my hairnet off. I nod at Lisa and I'm off like a shot. I zoom past Beverly and the armed guard. Their job is preventing people from getting in; they never pay attention to me when I'm exiting. The travel room is nearly sixty stories below my quarters, and I'm going farther than that, all the way to the roof. I sprint, taking the stairs two at a time.

When the metal door to the hall smacks open on the twenty-fifth floor, I'm so startled, I catch my foot on the top step and sprawl forward onto the landing, banging my right knee hard, but catching myself with the palms of my gloved hands. I look up, breathing heavily.

"Rosie! I've been looking everywhere for you." Sarah grabs my elbow and hauls me to my feet. "What on Earth are you wearing?"

I open my mouth, but she rushes on before I can speak. "No, never mind that. David needs you right now. You've got to get to your dad; there's no time to waste. Follow me."

Oh my god. Seriously, what is happening? What was the Achtung about? Sarah leads me toward the middle of the tower, where three elevator shafts pierce the center of the building from top to bottom. We call them the straws. Three giant, dark tubes filled with a hundred feet of filthy water at the bottom. Dad must be sending down a rappelling hook to winch me up to the roof. What could be so urgent about that Achtung he received that I had to bypass the seventieth floor stairwell landing security this way?

When I was a little kid, I was never allowed on the twenty-fifth floor because that's the only floor that has open access to the shafts. We don't have quarters or storage on twenty-five either; it's basically deserted. It's too dangerous.

"Come on. Hurry," Sarah says, racing ahead of me. She stops at the gaping maw of the southern shaft. "I'll help you with your hook."

I join her at the edge of the shaft and look up, hanging on to the frame with my right hand and reaching out for the grappling hook with my left. There's nothing there.

Sarah's breath is hot in my ear. "Two years waiting for you to come of age *is* a long time," she hisses. "I'm ready to get pregnant now." I try to whirl around, but she shoves me in the back, and I tumble forward, falling into a far different void than the one I'd planned for.

# CHAPTER FIVE

March 21, 2074

My training kicks in instantaneously. Columbia Tower is flooded to the tenth floor, so I only have seconds before I hit the water. I curl my knees toward my chest and try to wrap my arms around them, cannonball style. My body twists as my center of gravity rotates and I enter the water butt-first with a painful smack.

Plunging downward into the murky, fetid water of the elevator shaft seems to take even longer than my one-hundred-and-fifty-foot freefall drop. I'm disoriented, but I think I sense myself slowing, and I uncurl my legs and frog-kick as hard as I can to propel myself back up to the surface.

My eyes are shut tightly, and I swim headfirst into something metallic, probably a strut or support beam in the shaft. My head rocks and my neck screams with agony, but I keep kicking. Twenty excruciating seconds later, my face breaks the surface and I gulp gigantic breaths of air.

I bob in the putrid water for several moments until I get my breath back. Thank god we're trained from toddler age what to do during an accidental fall.

Accidental, my ass. Sarah's trying to kill me, to get me out of the way so she can have a child with my father. *"I'm ready to get pregnant now."* Her voice echoes in my head. Psycho bitch. I thought she was vapid and useless. I way underestimated her.

I'm treading water, and my foot connects painfully with flotsam below the surface. I have got to get out of here. I tread harder and tilt my head back. The tiny pinprick of light is the roof-level opening, and it's almost a thousand feet away. Still, I call out. "Dad! Daddy!" I scream, my voice ricocheting off the vertical walls of the shaft. How far will my sound waves travel before they peter out? I don't know the answer.

Lisa! Lisa and the hairy-armed guy are only ten or eleven floors above me. Beverly and the guard too. "Lisa!" I scream. "Anyone!" I call out over and over, my breath growing shorter as I struggle harder to keep myself afloat and shout at the same time. I lose my rhythm and my mouth dips below the waterline. Foul liquid pools into my mouth. I spit it out, gasping, and have the most painfully obvious thought of my life. This would be a lot easier to do if I had something to hang on to. I stop my stupid treading water and I swim to the side, feeling around in the blackness for the wall.

I find it, and there are struts or support beams or something, I don't know what, but it's a handhold and that's what I need right now. I scream for Dad, Lisa, anyone, over and over, for at least ten minutes, maybe more. I have no sense of time down here. But nobody responds. Lisa is probably tucked away in her control room, prepping for the next mission, or she's in her quarters, wherever they are. Beverly and the armed guard are nowhere near the straws, and the entrances are covered by steel sheeting on twenty-one anyway. Dad was probably never even here. No. Someone called the control room and got Lisa and the hairy-armed guy to abort the mission. Sarah doesn't even know about the time travel program. It couldn't have been her. But it came from our quarters, Lisa said so. Could Sarah have known more than I gave her credit for? She's already surprised me once, in the most horrible of ways.

I tread water for just a couple of seconds to give my arms a quick break. No one can hear me. Nobody is coming to my rescue. If I'm going to get out of here, I'm going to have to climb fifteen stories back to the landing on the twenty-fifth floor to do it. It's going to be the most important climb of my life.

I latch on to the support strut again, and I feel around with my feet, discovering crevices in the wall. The booties of my time travel outfit are actually perfect for this. I can curl my toes around the thinnest of edges.

Feeling a glimmer of hope, I begin to inch up the vertical shaft. My eyes have adjusted to the very dim light, and instead of pitch blackness, I see hazy shapes in shades of the darkest brown, but I'll take it. The closer I get to the twenty-fifth floor, the better I can see. The elevator shaft was constructed with crisscrossing exposed beams; it wasn't finished off with sheets of smooth metal. I send a little mental blessing of gratitude toward the long-dead builders and architects of this tower.

The ambient glow of the twenty-fifth floor now shines like the sun on a Burn Level Zero day. I'm twenty feet away.

Ten.

Five.

My fingertips curl around the lip of the twenty-fifth floor and I find a last toe hold, pushing my torso up a foot. I brace my right elbow on the floor and use my arms to lift my head and shoulders above floor level. My feet dangle in thin air now, my weight is all on my upper chest, but that's enough. I've made it. Wiggling the rest of my body onto the floor will be easy.

I pull myself forward to waist level and look up just in time to get kicked in the face. "How stupid do you think I am?" Sarah sneers. She stomps on my right shoulder with a heavy black boot.

"You think I'd just walk away from this? I've passed all my climbs too."

She pushes me backward until I'm hanging on by my gloved fingertips, my feet swaying below me, scrabbling but unable to find a toehold. I reach out and try to grab Sarah's ankle, but she darts sideways and stomps on my other hand. The tips of my fingers graze her boot and my pinkie loops through her shoelace. I lose my grip with my damaged hand, and I slide down a foot, my hand tangled in Sarah's boot. She's going to have to let me climb her, or she's coming with me.

I can't see her anymore – my head is below the lip of the floor – but she's screaming and her leg shakes violently. I have her in a death grip and I am not letting go. She writhes and kicks as I drag her struggling body closer to the edge, inch by inch.

Suddenly, she becomes as light as a feather, and I have a brief flash of hollow victory as I freefall. I'll drown her when we hit the bottom and then I'll try the climb again. I curl myself into a ball and cradle her empty boot against my body.

I'm still screaming with rage as I hit the water and sink back into its rotting depths.

# CHAPTER SIX

March 21, 2074

I bob back up to the surface and I don't mess around with treading water or yelling for help this time. I swim straight to the side, find a handhold, and I cry.

I know now that Sarah's going to wait up there on the twenty-fifth floor until she's sure I'm dead. I'm keenly aware of how severely I underestimated my father's wife.

I squeeze my eyes shut and I choke back my sobs. It's eerily silent down here once my breathing is calm. I hope Sarah couldn't hear me crying. I hope she thinks the fall broke me this time. Because there's one more way out of here, and if I make it, the first thing I'm going to do is haul myself back into Columbia Tower, find her, and kill her. But I have to go down to come back up.

My arms tremble. I can't delay. I don't have much strength left, and it won't be too many minutes before I slip below the surface, unable to hang on any longer. I take a deep breath and hold it. I use my epiglottis, the leaf-shaped flap of cartilage attached to the back of my tongue, to seal off my throat, then I pull another mouthful of air in, my cheeks puffing out as far as they'll go. Using my tongue like a kind of shovel, I push the mouthful of air down into my lungs while still holding my original lungful. I repeat that process over and over while I think.

We're flooded to the tenth floor. No matter which floor I try to exit, I'll be swimming blindly in the dark. Inside the building, the closer I am to the surface of the water, the worse the debris field will be, due to surface winds and currents. My best bet is ground level. I know from my trips to the past that Columbia Tower had a wide-open lobby with little furnishings and few barriers to the exterior walls.

I pack another lungful of air. This process is taking precious time, but I'm going to have to hold my breath for several minutes, so it's necessary. I'll have to swim down the elevator shaft until I touch the bottom, then hope the doors are gone or that I can force them open. Even just a few inches will be enough for me to slither through. I'll swim in one direction until I get some indication that I'm out of the building. Then I'll float up to the top.

I'm not the best among my littermates at packing my lungs and holding my breath. Not even close. The longest I've ever gone in the practice tank was six minutes and fourteen seconds. Boris holds the record for our litter, at nineteen minutes, two seconds. But I don't need that much time. I can swim ten stories down then out through the lobby in less than six minutes, I know it. One hundred feet down, maybe five hundred feet across. Totally doable.

Of course, in the practice tank, I hadn't been swimming through fifty years of accumulated junk and debris in the pitch dark, but I shove that thought aside just as I shove a final mouthful of air into my lungs. I flip my body and swim headfirst toward the bottom.

I stroke, pulling hard with my arms and using a forceful frog kick, but it's still way harder to swim down than it is to swim up. The pressure builds in my ears, so I know I'm definitely getting deeper.

It's black as mold down here, and I try to keep my eyes shut, but every once in a while they pop open reflexively, my brain insisting this time I'll see something, so each time I'm startled again by how black and sightless it is. I brush against a few pieces of flotsam, but miraculously I don't get snagged on anything.

I've been swimming at least two minutes when my gloved hand brushes the bottom. My lungs aren't burning yet, but there's definitely a huge difference between holding my breath in the tank and doing it while swimming in a free dive with my life on the line. I have, at most, four minutes left in me. A little bit of luck now would be more than welcome.

And unbelievably, I get some. Striking out blindly in the direction I think is most likely to be the elevator door, my left arm reaches forward a couple feet while my right shoulder bumps into an edge. I've found the door on my first try, and it's jammed open at least a foot. I can get through that. I pivot my body to a 'standing' position and slip through the crack in the elevator door. Then I swim for all I'm worth in total darkness, using ten powerful strokes to take me straight away from the elevator doors. I swim directly into a wall. A little bit of breath bursts accidentally from my lungs and I curse myself. I can't afford a mistake like that. I swim slower now, trailing my hand against the wall, and I can tell when I get to a corner of the building because one wall meets another and I pivot ninety degrees to swim and search for an exit along that wall.

I'm on the first floor, I must be, and from what I know of the building there should be at least one wall that's mostly doors to the outside. Once I find that, I'll swim through and then zoom to the surface. My lungs are beginning to complain. It won't be long before the complaint turns to a burn, and then a desperate and uncontrollable desire to breathe. But I haven't found the doors yet. My fingers find something that feels like a rubber seal, but it can't be a seal because it moves a little. It must be a door! I push hard, and it moves even more. I push and swim, but it never seems to stop, and I can't tell if I'm outside or not. I swear I just went around in a complete circle. *Revolving door*, my brain supplies. I want to cry. Did I go all the way around in a complete circle? If I exit the door now, am I back inside the building? Will I swim twenty feet upward only to hit my head on a cathedral ceiling? *Stupid, stupid, stupid.*

My lungs have gone from complaining to angry. I don't have much more time. My eyes open again of their own accord, and this time it's not a useless exercise. I look back and forth, and yes! The water behind me is the inky black of obsidian, but the water in front of me is a lighter shade of black, like the color of pencil lead. The tiniest bit of light is filtering down from the surface. The exit must be straight ahead. I keep my eyes open now and swim forward directly into a wall of sunken debris piled against the outside of the building. All I can do is try to swim and pick my way through it and do my best to get closer to the surface.

The water is murky and greenish black, and I know I'm outside and away from the building, but I still can't see well enough to truly navigate. All I can do is swim the path of least resistance. Though all I want to do is go up, break the surface, and take a breath, sometimes I'm blocked, and I have to swim down again to find my way around or through whatever detritus is obstructing my path. My lungs are screeching at me now. I don't know anymore how long I've been down here. There's a good chance I've broken my personal best, but it's no cause to celebrate because the water is still the color of seaweed, and I've reached an area where I can't seem to go up, down, or forward due to a debris blockage. I'm backtracking when I'm yanked to a halt. One of the pockets of my jacket has gotten hooked on something, a knob or a spur of metal, I don't know, but I struggle with it, trying to free myself, but I only seem to become more entangled. I try to unzip my jacket, but the zipper jams halfway. My lungs give a howl of agony, and a blast of breath bursts out of my mouth. That's it. I'm going to die. I'm out of oxygen, and I'm out of time.

*Time.*

Underwater, in the greenish bracken, my eyes widen. Time. I gave my travel chemicals back to the hairy-armed man when my mission was aborted. But only the departure half. I still have the half meant for my return trip in my vest pocket.

Desperately trying not to gulp in a deep lungful of seawater, I draw my helmet out of my inner vest pocket and swish it down over my head. I'll never get it Velcroed to my collar, so I just fasten the side clamps and cinch them down as tightly as I can. I unzip the access panel to my port-a-cath. I won't be able to peel up my second skin with this glove on. I take it off and let it float away. I peel back the second skin and try not to be completely grossed out knowing the filthy floodwaters are pouring into my open port. I unzip my return hypodermic and flick the protective nub off the tip. Did I plunge a little of the chemicals out just now? I may have. It was calibrated for a sixty-seven year trip. If I wasted some just now, where will I end up? I have no time to stop and worry about it.

I force the tip of the hypodermic into my seawater flooded port-a-cath. Spots bloom in front of my eyes from lack of oxygen.

*Plunge.* I jam my thumb down on the hypodermic, thrusting the chemicals into my bloodstream.

*Withdraw.* I whip the needle back out.

*Drop.* I open my hand, and the spent hypodermic floats into the abyss.

*Slap.* Slap? Confusion is taking over. Oh…right. I reapply my second skin over the open port-a-cath, but it's too wet and won't stick.

*Zip.* Zip? I don't know what that means. The spots in front of my eyes grow so large they seem to burst into a shower of black glitter, and I slip into something. Whether it's death or the void, I do not know.

# PART II
# JUNE 19, 2018

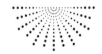

*Thud.*

"What the hell?" a guy's voice yells. Canvas writhes and flaps as two dirty teenage boys in stained clothing worm out of the collapsed tent.

A third boy sitting cross-legged on the sidewalk stares at them with round, unfocused eyes. "Holy shit, dude. Some chick just fell out of the sky."

"Jesus!" The blond boy from the tent rakes his hand through his already messy, longish hair and stares at the pile of canvas and poles askew on the sidewalk. "Come on, Carlos," he says, prodding his tall, dark-haired companion. "Help me pull her outta there."

The boys wade into the billowing canvas of the collapsed tent. The blond boy reaches in, grasps the girl by the shoulders, flips her over, then jumps back. "Oh, crap, dude."

Behind him, Carlos cranes his neck to see. "What?"

"This isn't some chick. It's Lita, Jimmy Squint's girl."

"I thought she went to juvie?"

"I guess she's out and crashing our tent. Literally."

Carlos steps closer and peers at her. "I don't know, Dez. I think she's too short to be Lita."

"How can you tell how tall she is when she's lying down?" Dez leans over her. "Lita? Hey, Lita, it's Dez. Remember me? Wake up." The girl's eyelids flutter. She moans and throws her hands over her face.

Dez turns to Carlos. "Dude, she's soaking wet. What is she wearing? That some kind of new juvie jumpsuit? You don't think she escaped, do you?"

Carlos shakes his head. "Nah. No telling what she's gotten up to, though, or what she's coming down off of."

The girl turns her head, retches, and coughs up a gallon of what looks like seawater and puke mixed together, and the boys jump back.

"Ah, man! The tent. Crap, what the hell, Lita?" Dez yells. He raises his hand as if to slap her upside the head, but Carlos grabs it.

"Knock it off, dude," Carlos says. "Let's get her off the tent, fix the poles, and drag her inside where she can sleep it off."

"I'm not bringing that thing in my tent."

"What do you think Jimmy Squint's gonna say when he finds out you left his girl dope-sick and out on the street?"

Dez glares at Carlos, then his shoulders sag. "You hold her arms. I'll get her legs."

Carlos lifts her easily under her armpits. Dez struggles with her legs. Lurching, they move her off the tent and place her on the sidewalk. "You stay here with her, make sure nobody messes with her. I'll fix the tent," Carlos says.

It only takes him a minute or two to pop the poles back up and get the tent shaped back into a dome. Passersby hurrying between office buildings avert their eyes. One makes a snide remark under his breath about the homeless, and how the sidewalks are for taxpayers, but Carlos and Dez ignore him, and the girl's too out of it to notice. Her eyes are closed; the only indication she's alive is the slight flutter of the pulse in her neck.

Carlos and Dez drag her inside the tent, stuff a couple of wadded-up sweatshirts under her head, and lay a threadbare sleeping bag over her. She clenches and releases her right fist several times, then shivers, rolls onto one side, and lies as still as the dead.

## CHAPTER SEVEN

June 21, 2018

I peel my eyes open. I'm in a darkened enclosure, but I'm not alone. The air isn't pitch black. I see the outlines of at least two other people lying curled on either side of me. The ground beneath me is hard. When I wiggle my body, every nerve ending reports sharp pain, but I can barely filter that information through the pounding in my head, which is the worst feeling of all.

There's quick movement to my right. "Hey, whozat...what's going...?" A boy speaks, but he cuts himself off. "Hey, you're awake," he says, so quietly I almost can't hear him over the screaming pain in my head.

"Drink," I croak.

"Yeah, here you go." He hands me a half full jug.

I lift my head a couple inches, unscrew the cap, and drink a long sip of the most deliriously delicious water I've ever tasted. I glug another swig.

"Slow down or you might puke again."

I sigh and hand him the bottle. "Thanks," I say, my voice less scratchy than before. I close my eyes and lie back down.

"You're welcome," the boy whispers. "Do you remember me?"

I open one eye. "I don't think so."

"I'm Carlos. You're Lita, right?"

Lita. There's something familiar about that. "Um…" I say. "That sounds kind of right."

"Somebody slipped you some bad shit, Lita. Maybe fentanyl? You've been asleep for two days. Don't worry, though. We'll take care of you until we can hook you back up with Jimmy."

"Who's Jimmy?"

Carlos waits a couple of beats before responding. "Jimmy. Your boyfriend. He's, uh…well, you should probably remember who he is before he comes looking for you."

I shrug, my shoulders raising the sleeping bag I'm huddled under just a little. "Okay, I'll try." I think hard for a couple minutes. "I'm pretty sure I have some other things to do too."

"Can one of them be shut the hell up and go back to sleep?" a cranky voice on the other side of me whines.

Now that I've quenched my thirst, I feel like I could sleep for a million years. I don't respond. I just pull the covers over my head, curl into the fetal position, and pass out again immediately.

---

Strange noises wake me up, but it's not the boys in the tent. The sounds aren't completely foreign, but they're hard to identify. Squeals, grinds, metallic clunking sounds, and a steadily growing whirring hum of constant activity draw me out of my sleeping bag, through the canvas flap, and onto the sidewalk.

It's no longer night time; a yellowish-gray light has broken over the city. My brain expects to see water everywhere, but there isn't a drop of it in sight. My neurons scramble and reorder themselves to the reality of gray concrete, pedestrians, and two-

and four-wheeled vehicles cruising past in both directions, up and down the hill my tent is pitched on.

"What is all this?" I whisper out loud.

The flap rustles behind me, and I turn to see a dark-haired boy emerging. "Good morning," he says.

"Carlos?"

He nods.

"Did you give me a drink of water last night?"

"It was warm, but at least we had some."

"It tasted like it's never been reclaimed."

Carlos gives me a funny look, tilting his head to the side. "You feeling okay, Lita?"

I flex my fingers and toes, then look down at my feet. "What are these things?" I say, gesturing to the booties on my feet.

"You tell me. They look like hospital slippers. Is that where you came from? Dez thought you went to juvie."

"Juvie?" My heart pounds. "It's flooded there. Way too dangerous."

Carlos chuckles and pretends to shadow box. "It's way less dangerous now that you're outta there, right?" He turns and motions for me to follow him. "Come on. Let's get some breakfast."

He starts to walk downhill, but every nerve in my body screams 'danger' and I stay rooted to the spot. He looks back at me. "You coming?"

My eyes must be wide with panic. I shake my head. "Could we go uphill?"

He shrugs. "Pioneer Square's usually a better bet than Pill Hill, but if you feel that strong about it, I guess so."

My body sags with relief, and I don't even know why I was so tense in the first place, but I'm grateful to Carlos for being so easygoing. "Downhill just feels really dangerous," I say.

Carlos nods sagely. "You always gotta listen to your sixth sense. I tell everybody, you get that feeling, that prickle on your neck, whatever, that tells you something isn't right, you gotta listen to it. That's your animal instinct coming out. That's evolution. Too many people ignore that voice."

We begin moving uphill. I'm so hungry that my head hurts. My eyes scan left and right, looking for nourishment, and I hit the jackpot almost immediately. "Over there!" I cry, pointing and running to a spot where the sidewalk meets the edge of a brick building. I reach down, grasp a handful of green leaves, and pull. The entire dandelion lifts from its crevice, and I laugh in delight. I pluck off two of the leaves and stuff them in my mouth. It's heavenly. I pop off the flowerhead and suck the juice out of the stem before a hand clasps my shoulder and pulls me backward a step.

"Lita, what are you doing?"

I'm immediately ashamed. It was like an animal inside me took over. "I'm sorry. I was just so hungry. I should have shared. I'll help you look, and the next one is all yours."

Carlos's mouth drops open in disbelief.

I brush loose dirt off my fingertips and hold my fingers in a V. "The next two."

Carlos throws back his head and laughs long and loud. "You're as crazy as Old Dirty P!"

I smile uncertainly. Carlos slings an arm around my shoulders. "You had me going for a minute, Lita. I didn't know you were so funny. I wasn't sure about this at first, but I might be glad you picked our tent to crash. Come on."

Carlos leads me up the hill, and even though we pass at least a dozen more wild dandelions – *what is this magical place?* – I don't stop to dine. My immediate hunger is sated, and I'm curious to find out what Carlos has in mind.

We're not alone. Other people walk the streets as well. They walk with purpose, like Carlos, as if they all have places to be. Their destinations must be important because not one of them stops to gather any of the manna I see everywhere.

We cross beneath something like a concrete lid, and the noise level rises dramatically. When we emerge from under the lid, the noise decreases and the sunlight is dazzling. Carlos tugs on my elbow, pulling me off the sidewalk and onto a narrow little side street between buildings.

"You in the mood for Thai?"

*Tie?* I shrug noncommittally.

"There's a place at the end of this block that's only open dinner hours. Probably something good and maybe no hassle."

I nod, absolutely no idea what he's talking about, and follow him down the narrow street, which is blocked at the end by a large green metal container. Carlos approaches it and whacks it with the side of his hand. "Dammit!" he exclaims.

"What?"

He jiggles the lid up and down a couple inches. "Dumpster's padlocked! Jerks!" He kicks the base. "Like it's really going to hurt anyone. It's garbage! It should be fair game!"

I look at the simple combination lock that seems to have Carlos so perplexed. "You want to get in there?" I ask.

"Yeah, but apparently they're smuggling priceless antiques from the Ming Dynasty in there. It's off-limits."

Carlos hasn't been making sense for a while now, but if he wants to see what's inside the big locked box, I know I want to help him, and somehow, I'm sure I can.

He crosses his arms, huffs in exasperation, and begins to walk back down the narrow street, but I don't follow. Instead, I walk to the big lockbox, flip the combination lock so that I can press my ear against it, and I begin to spin the dial.

"What are you doing?" Carlos asks.

"Shh," I admonish. "Now I need to start over."

I shake the lock in my hand, position it against my ear again, and turn the dial once more. The lock behaves as if it's brand new. The clicks, clinks, and tumbling noises are so loud, I could probably do this without having it pressed against my ear. Two revolutions to the right, one to the left, and a half twist to the right, and the lock springs open in my hand when I yank down. I unlace it from the metal closures it had been holding together. I gesture to Carlos, who's still several feet away from me. "Here you go," I call out.

Carlos's mouth is open in an 'O.' "Dude, you just cracked that in like fifteen seconds."

I'm not sure if he's being critical or not – his tone is inscrutable – so I hedge my bets with my response. "It went pretty smoothly, but maybe I could do it faster next time."

His lips quirk up into a grin. "Lita, you are something else."

Something else besides what, I'm not sure, but he's smiling and it gives me such a warm, happy feeling that I smile back. The muscles in my face ache, like they're not used to doing this.

Carlos lifts the lid on the box, and the aromas that erupt from it hit me so hard, I stagger a step.

His grin hasn't left his face. "Jackpot!" he exclaims. He reaches in and pulls out a large black bag. He loosens the ties on it to open it all the way, revealing a cornucopia of treats the likes of which I've never seen.

"Is that all edible?" I breathe.

"Most of it. I'm not a big fan of yam naem, but with enough peanut sauce, anything tastes good. Haven't you had Thai?"

"I don't think so. Maybe. I don't know."

He roots around in the bag, finds a plastic spoon, and dips it into a sauce. "Here, this looks like red curry. Try it."

I place the spoonful in my mouth and the flavors explode across my tongue in a riot so intense, it brings tears to my eyes.

"Spicy?" Carlos asks.

I wipe a tear away while I roll the food around in my mouth, letting it hit every part of my tongue. "Can I have more?"

"Let's take it back to the tent. We'll share with Dez and you can have as much as you like."

I understand now why the box was locked. I can't wrap my

mind around how valuable this must be. I dart my gaze up and down the alley. "Are you sure? What if we're followed? Somebody has to be watching us."

"Nah, this place is only open dinner hours, like I said. We'll put the lock back on; they'll never even know we were here. We're not leaving a mess or anything. Could you pop that lock again if you had to?"

"Yeah," I say. "Anytime."

Carlos smiles at me again. "I wish we were gonna hang together longer. I'll be sorry to see you go when Jimmy turns up to collect you."

I smile uncertainly. He keeps talking about this Jimmy person, but I have absolutely no memory of him. In fact, on a quick scan, I don't have thoughts or recollections about anything, really. All I want to do right now is consume the food Carlos has hefted over his shoulder. The amazing smells coming from the black bag almost make me forget my pounding headache. I'm still holding the lock to the metal box, so I close the lid and lace it back through the holes that line up in the metal, and I snap the lock shut. "Let's eat," I say. This time, on our way back down the hill, I note the locations of the multiple dandelion outcroppings we pass, but I don't regret leaving them behind. I know where they are, and despite the fact that the sidewalks are now crawling with other people, no one has harvested them. I can come back for them later. If that black bag is as stuffed full of food as I think it might be, I might not even have to.

---

At the tent, my fantasies turn into reality. The bag is heaped with food, and it's not just the dish Carlos called red curry. There are piles and piles of edible items that I don't have names for. Some of them even come in little paper boxes with folding tabs and thin metal handles. There are long wiggly items that Carlos and Dez call noodles. I take in everything without much comment, loading the vocabulary into my brain. I instinctively know that I can't show my ignorance. Noodles, chicken, beef, curry, peanut, and more. I sample flavors and commit the nouns Carlos and Dez use to describe them to memory. Some of the words ring faint bells, but most of them are totally new.

After we finish eating, I lay back on the blankets and sleeping bags and rub my tummy. This sense of satiation feels unfamiliar, like I've never been truly stuffed full of food before. It's wonderful. My headache has receded into a totally manageable mild pain at the base of my skull.

"You look different, Lita," Carlos comments. "Thai suits you."

"I feel better," I say. "I had a really bad headache before."

"You never said nothing." Dez leans back, rummages in a pile, and pulls out a white plastic bottle. "I have some Tylenol."

"Oh, thanks, but I'm okay now." I'm not sure what Tylenol is, but like the other new terms I've absorbed, I can tell it's something a normal person should know, so I keep my ignorance to myself.

"We should probably look into getting you something else to wear," Carlos says. He fingers the sleeve of my jacket. "This is still wet. Not soaking anymore, but it's not gonna dry all the way until you air it out. I don't think we've got anything that would fit you, though. How tall are you?"

I shrug. "I'm not sure."

"Step outside with me for a minute. Come on, Dez. You too."

We all exit the tent and Carlos has me and Dez stand back to back. "Dang, you're short," Carlos says to me.

"I am not," I fire back. I take a peek back at Dez and see that I'm about eye level with his shoulder. "He's a giant."

"He's five-foot-eight." Carlos laughs. "And you're straight outta *The Wizard of Oz*, right up to the part where you fell on our house."

"Dorothy fell on the house. She wasn't a Munchkin," Dez corrects.

"Nobody fell on a house, a house fell on them. I said it wrong," Carlos replies.

I massage my temples, feeling a tiny thread of headache inching its way upward. "I'm not a Munchkin and my name's not Dorothy," I say. "Why are we even doing this? What does it matter how tall I am?"

Carlos grins and holds up his hands. "You're five feet of fury, Lita. Maybe four-eleven. And there's nothing wrong with that. It just means you can't borrow anything from us without looking like you just climbed out of a clown car. But that's easy enough to fix when you know the right people." He snaps his fingers. "Dez," he says authoritatively, "hold down the fort. Me and Lita are gonna pop some tags."

It's way easier for Carlos to talk me into walking downhill when I have a full stomach, but it still makes me nervous. But I do it because unlike me, Carlos seems totally sure of himself.

And nothing bad happens. I don't know what I expect, but my heart races like crazy with each step downhill, and I'm glad when we turn left on a street marked with a sign that reads, "4th Ave." Fourth Ave also seems to be taking us gradually downhill, but I can handle it better than the first steep hill, where it felt like I was racing straight into the open, waiting arms of doom.

Carlos walks beside me, his arms swinging loosely. "Just so you know, I'm not actually planning to pop tags. I don't steal."

"Me neither," I say with conviction. I don't know much about anything right now, and it feels good to respond so decisively and automatically.

"Really?" Carlos says. "I didn't know that. No offense, but I guess I had you pegged wrong."

"I'm not offended," I say, even though a part of me kind of is. Now that my headache has mostly worn off, I've had a chance to think, and what I'm coming up with is scaring me. Because I'm drawing a blank. About virtually everything. I think Lita's my name, but I don't know for sure. I believe I'm sixteen, but I don't know why. I'm not sure how I ended up in Carlos and Dez's tent, or how I got there, or why I was apparently soaking wet. And when I search my mind, I feel like I'm trying to walk backward across a long expanse of pure white nothingness. I don't remember anything. Maybe if I can get Carlos talking about me, I'll start to recognize myself through his assumptions. "Why did you think I'd be a thief?"

"It sounds really bad when you say it that way," Carlos mumbles beside me.

"Like I said, I'm not mad. I'm just curious."

"Well... you're Jimmy Squint's girl. So I figured you were more like him." He trails his fingers along the brick wall of the building we're walking next to. "And you live in The Jungle. Me and Dez, we stay outta there. It's no picnic living on James Street, we take a lot of shit from the bourgeois, but it's better than being around all the drugs and the crap that goes down where you're at."

I still don't recognize the name Jimmy Squint, and 'The Jungle' means nothing to me. I walk along in silence, trying to think of another question I can ask him that will get him to tell me stuff about myself without revealing my own ignorance when Carlos stops in a doorway and starts addressing a large pile of debris. "Hey, Old Dirty!" He crouches down and prods the pile of garbage, which shifts and groans.

"Is that a person?" I blurt out.

"It's ODP," Carlos nods. "Old Dirty Plastered? You don't know him?"

I shake my head.

"I thought everybody knew him. How long have you been on the streets?"

I shrug. "A while."

He turns back and shakes the lump by its shoulder. "Dirty? We call him Ol' Dirty after... Well, never mind. You probably don't know him, either."

He gets down on his hands and knees and lifts a sheet of newspaper, revealing a bulbous nose and a chin covered with long, scraggly gray hair. "Dirty? You okay in there?"

I can't quite make out the mumbled reply, but Carlos pats the man's shoulder area. "Gonna be a hot one today. I'm leaving you some water. It's right here by your head, okay?" Carlos reaches into a pocket of his cargo shorts, pulls out a plastic bottle of water, and sets it on the sidewalk.

There's another mumble, and a tan hand with filthy, torn fingernails slides out of the pile of fabric and papers, snatches the bottle, and retreats.

Carlos rises. "You take care, Dirty." He crooks his finger at me. "C'mon."

We walk a few feet away before I speak. "Is he, like, your friend?"

"ODP is a fixture. He doesn't have friends. I'm really surprised you don't know him."

"Maybe I know him by some other name."

"Yeah, right." Carlos laughs. "You probably call him Bill Gates."

I totally do not understand Carlos's sense of humor, but at least I've gotten to know him well enough that I can tell he's joking with me, so I smile back.

"I have General Gates on the comm, can I put him through?" I reply. I have no idea where that comes from, but Carlos laughs.

"Old Dirty's a loon. He must have done some real bad drugs in the sixties. I would say he's harmless, but I know for a fact he's not. It worked out in my favor, though, so I'm not complaining."

"What happened?"

Carlos kicks a rock on the sidewalk, and it skitters down the street. "One night I got a little too close to the edge of The Jungle, and I was by myself. Not too far from here, now that I think about it. Anyway, it was late at night, and a few guys came up and started shaking me down. I didn't have anything to give them, they got pissed, and next thing I know, I'm on the ground and I'm getting kicked in the face."

I shudder, and I think somehow, I know exactly how that felt. "That's awful."

"Yeah. I don't know what would have happened – maybe they would have given up when I blacked out or maybe they would have killed me – but all of a sudden that crazy bastard drops out of the sky, lands right on one of the guys, and beats the living crap out of all three of them."

"He fell out of the sky?"

"Well, not really. ODP likes to climb; you'll see him all over the city climbing stuff. Climbed a tree in Westlake Center once around Christmas, shut the whole damn block down for hours – it was awesome. You see him on fire escapes a lot. Like that one over there."

Carlos points across the street to a brick building with a ton of windows, row after row of them. It has a metal staircase clinging to the outside of the brick façade, with a small landing at each window level. The apparatus ends in a ladder that hangs about six feet above the ground.

"A staircase on the outside of the building," I marvel. "What an interesting idea."

Carlos crosses his eyes at me. We've reached a corner, and we wait, I think because there's a glowing red hand on the other side of the street. Sure enough, when it changes to a glowing white person shape, Carlos steps off the curb, so I follow. "Yeah, so, ODP happened to be on the fire escape above us when I was getting my ass handed to me, and he jumped those bastards right back and made them sorry they'd ever laid eyes on me. I've had a soft spot for him ever since."

Carlos veers off the sidewalk and into a driveway that leads to a large one-story building with the word 'Goodwill' written across it in letters multiple feet high. "Let's go around back," Carlos says. "I know a guy."

The guy Carlos knows has sallow skin, is several inches shorter than him, and very skinny. He smiles nervously, but I don't get the sense that he's worried. I think that's just his natural look. "Hey, man," he says, slapping hands with Carlos.

"Hey, Kevin," Carlos replies.

"Who's your friend?" Kevin asks, eyeing me up and down.

"Dude, it's Lita. You know, Jimmy Squint's girl?"

Kevin's eyes widen and he takes a half step back. "That ain't Lita."

Full as it is, my stomach seems to get even heavier, and I feel it drop several inches.

Carlos looks at me sidelong, his hands stuffed in the pockets of his cargo shorts. "Well, that's the name she answers to."

"Some other Lita maybe." Kevin narrows his eyes appraisingly. "This chick's hair is darker. And she's a few inches too short to be Jimmy's Lita." He turns to me. "I wouldn't go around pretending to be somebody you're not. Especially *that* somebody."

I wrap my arms around my stomach, which is really starting to hurt. The name Lita had sounded so familiar when Carlos and Dez called me that. Why couldn't it be my name? I wasn't trying to be somebody else. I wasn't even sure who I was, so how could I pretend to be some other person?

I look at Carlos, and maybe it's panic in my eyes or the pain from the knot in my stomach, but he sees something in my face that he takes pity on, and he slings his arm around my shoulder. "Well, this Lita is an amazing little lockpicker, and I kinda hope I don't have to give her back to Jimmy Squint because I might want to keep her around." He squeezes me to his side briefly before releasing me. "Her clothes are trashed, though. She crashed into our tent the other night soaking wet and covered in seaweed."

I hadn't heard about the seaweed part. I'd shown up with food all over me? Then how could have I have been so hungry this morning? Nothing made sense, and a stabbing pain in my neck joined the ache in my belly.

"She needs new clothes," Carlos says. "Can you help a brother out?"

Kevin shrugs and angles his head at a row of huge metal boxes. "I got two containers full of donations I ain't logged in yet. Go through 'em and take whatever you want."

Carlos smiles. "Thanks, man. I won't forget it."

Kevin darts his nervous grin back. "It's cool."

Carlos and I cross over to a couple of huge cardboard boxes. He roots around and pulls out a few things but tosses them back in.

A flash of red catches my eye, and I reach in and draw out a filmy red dress. I hold it up to myself. It's completely impractical. I know the fabric would snag and get caught on anything I tried to climb, but I rub the slippery material between my fingers and unexpected tears spring to my eyes. "I want this one."

I dab at the tears with the hem of the skirt, and either Carlos doesn't notice I'm crying or he pretends not to see. "Good. Nice and light for hot weather. Let's see if we can find you some jeans too. And God!" He looks at my feet. "I forgot you had nothing on but those freaking paper slippers. Damn, you need some shoes."

He thrusts his hands back into the box, rummaging around, sorting, glancing at me, and discarding options. "What size shoes to you wear, anyway?"

Before I have a chance to tell him I don't know, he thrusts a pair of sneakers at me. "Try these."

I sit down, slip off my booties, and tug on the shoes. They're like boats on each foot. "They might work."

"Are you kidding me? You need something you can run in. Give 'em back."

I hand them over and he peels back the tongue and peers at it. "Dang, these are a kids' size four. Unbelievable." He keeps digging around in the box and I let him.

Kevin lets me go inside the back door of the building, and I use the bathroom inside and change my clothes. I take off my jacket. When I remove my vest, a three-inch-long flap of dirty beige tape comes with it, revealing some sort of device implanted in my skin. I don't know what it is, but I know instinctively that it's not normal. I crowd close to the scratched and dented mirror in the tiny bathroom. Fluid leaks from around the device, and it's a hub for red lines that radiate into my skin from around it. I snatch the T-shirt Carlos selected for me off the floor and pull it over my head, grateful to cover up that awful-looking thing. I stare at myself in the mirror. My hair is messy. I squeeze a lock and it feels crispy, like it might break off in my fingertips. My eyes look yellowish and my skin is pale, with just a bit of pink blotchiness in my cheeks. I place both palms on the mirror and lean forward until my nose is almost touching the pane. "What happened to you?" I whisper. "Who are you?"

I emerge from the bathroom in a pair of black jeans that are a little too big. Carlos says unless they make a size negative one, they'll have to do. I wear a bright green T-shirt and a pair of black sneakers that close with Velcro. The dress that made me cry is tied around my waist, because even though I'm not wearing it right now, I'm keeping it. Carlos shakes his head in bemusement but doesn't try to stop me. I thread the vest I've been wearing through one of my belt loops and let it dangle like a tattered flag. The rest of my old clothes get thrown into a black plastic bag with drawstrings like the one that held the Thai food.

Carlos says 'they're not even good enough for homeless people, and that's saying something'…whatever that means.

Carlos says he's hungry again, so we walk a couple of blocks until we find another one of the metal bins and I quickly manipulate the lock and pop it open. Everything smells exotic, but not as wonderful as before, probably because I still have a stomachache, which is getting worse. Carlos grabs a container that I know the name for. The word 'Styrofoam' pops right into my brain when I see the slightly spongy white clamshell.

"Aren't you going to eat?" Carlos asks.

"No, food doesn't sound good right now."

"You're a strange one, Lita. I always eat when I get the chance. Of course, with your skills" – Carlos twirls an imaginary dial – "I guess you don't have as much to worry about."

I smile queasily.

The walk back to the tent in some ways seems to take forever but also passes in the blink of an eye. My head is pounding and I pay little attention to my surroundings. Carlos whistles an off-key melody as we approach the tent that must be a signal. Dez pokes his head out.

"What took you so long?" His eyes fall on me, and his brow furrows. "Jeez, Lita, you don't look so good."

I sway a little and welcome the need to drop to my hands and knees to crawl into the tent. I pull myself over to a pile of clothing and blankets and burrow in. My eyes are open bare slits; the light hurts all the way to the back of my skull. Dez crawls in the tent, followed closely by Carlos.

"Is she okay?" I hear Carlos ask Dez.

"I dunno. I think so," he replies. "We're gonna be in for a world of hurt if she gets sicker on our watch. I don't want to be around when Jimmy comes for her."

"Yeah," Carlos agrees. "About that…"

Dez cuts him off. "Lita. Hey, Lita?"

I want to answer with words, but I croak an unintelligible response instead.

I sense movement next to me, and I feel a hand on my forehead. "She's burning up," Carlos says worriedly.

"Crap." Dez's voice is more scared than concerned. "Did you make sure she drank a bunch of water? She's coming down off some serious shit."

"She's acting *sick*, not dopesick."

My heart feels like it's pounding twice as fast as normal when Carlos presses a bottle of water into my hand. "Drink this. You'll feel a lot better. You need to change into cooler clothes too. It's too hot out for jeans when you have a fever. I guess that dress you grabbed was a good idea. Put it on. Come on, Dez. Let's give her some privacy for a couple minutes."

Oh, god. How am I going to do this? My arms and legs feel like lead, but I wriggle out of my jeans, force myself to a sitting position, and drag my green T-shirt over my head. Next, I try to slip into the silky read dress. Somehow, my head and right arm go through the correct holes, but my left arm can't find its way. I've used up all my energy; I have nothing remaining in the tank to care. I flop back down on the blanket pile.

"You ready?" Carlos says.

I whimper loud enough for him to hear me.

He comes back into the tent, takes one look at me, and his mouth drops open. "Oh, damn, Lita, you *are* sick, aren't you?"

My eyes drift closed, and his voice grows more urgent. "Dez, you've gotta help me get her to the hospital."

"She's just jonesin'," Dez says. "No way."

"I don't think that's it," Carlos says.

I feel his gentle touch on my shoulder, and his finger drifts to my collarbone, hovering near the weeping device in my chest. "Lita? Do you have cancer?"

Just like most of the things he's asked me about myself, I have no answer, so it's almost a good thing that I choose that moment to faint.

———

Whenever I try to open my eyes, the light burns. Words and phrases filter into my brain, mostly female voices.

"Temp is 104.9."

"My god, will you look at that thing? That has to come out."

"She's septic. We're admitting her."

"Sir, if you're going to be in the room, please stay out of our way."

Carlos's voice. "I think she might have cancer."

"Run a CBC. And get me a toxicology. We need to know what she's on."

Carlos again. "I don't think she's on anything."

"Of course she's not." Even in the depths of my delirium, I can hear the sarcasm thick in that voice.

"What did you take, sweetie? I need to know so I can help you. Do you speak English?"

Carlos's voice is sharp. "Yes, she speaks English. Jesus."

The female ignores him. "Where are you from, honey?"

Disjointed thoughts float in my brain like soap bubbles, and one of them pops. "Columbia," I rasp deliriously.

"Colombia?" Carlos asks. "Did she say Colombia?"

"Sir, I told you to stay out of our way. There's a chair in the corner."

Somebody grabs my hand but I don't think it's Carlos because they're not being gentle. My arm twists and a needle pokes into me. I almost manage to open my eyes to see what's going on, but then a rushing feeling floods through my body, and my brain turns itself off.

# CHAPTER EIGHT

June 23, 2018

A light clattering and the rustling sounds of movement awakens me, but I don't open my eyes.

"You're lucky she's not 'nothing by mouth,'" a woman's voice says in a light teasing tone. "Where would you be without room service?"

"You guys keep bringing her food even though she's asleep. What do you expect me to do?" Carlos asks, but he doesn't sound mad.

"If you're staying the night again, I can page housekeeping and see if we've freed up an extra cot yet."

"That would be great, thanks."

I wait until I hear the soft click of a door before I crack open one eye. Carlos is sitting in a corner of the room, his feet up, staring up at a television mounted on the wall and spooning food off a tray.

"Hey." My voice has obviously gone unused for a while. The word comes out in a whisper.

Carlos drops his plastic spoon and his feet swing to the floor.

"You're awake." He gives me a giant smile. "Oh, crap, your food. Here." He thrusts the spoon in my direction. "This is yours."

I chuff out a tired little laugh. "No, go ahead. I'm not hungry."

Carlos smiles, shyer this time. Setting the tray on a window ledge, he pulls his chair over next to my bed and leans his forearms on the mattress but doesn't touch me.

"How are you feeling?" he asks. "I mean, besides not hungry."

I take quick stock, along with a deep breath. My lungs are clear, and it's weird because I hadn't realized how heavy and liquidy my chest had felt until the sensation was gone. "Breathing doesn't hurt anymore," I say.

"Yeah, they said you had a lot of fluid in your lungs. Like, so much you almost dry-land drowned." Carlos points at one of the tubes that ends in a needle in my hand. "They're giving you IV antibiotics."

"Did they say what was wrong with me?"

"You had a really bad infection around your port. You got blood poisoning and the infection spread to other parts of your body. Your temperature was to the stratosphere and your kidneys were about to shut down. It was pretty bad."

"Wow."

"Yeah, but look at you, two days of sleep and antibiotics and you kicked it. You're tough as nails, Lita."

It's the first time he's said my name since I woke up, and the smile slides off my face. Lita isn't my name. I'm sure of it. But the trouble is, I still have no idea who I am. "Carlos?"

He knows I'm upset, and his hand reaches tentatively toward mine and rests lightly on top of my fingers. "What's up?"

"I don't think I'm who you think I am."

Carlos nods. "I don't think you are, either. You're way too sweet."

I feel a blush rise up my cheeks. That is not what I expected him to say. I'd thought he'd drop my hand, wish me all the best, and walk out the door. Instead he scoots an inch closer in his chair and squeezes two of my fingers lightly. "So, who are you?" he asks.

"That's the trouble," I whisper. "I honestly can't remember."

"A couple of nights ago, when you were in the ER, you told one of the nurses you were from Colombia."

The hairs on the back of my neck stand up, and I feel the truth of that statement. "Yeah," I say. "I am." A shudder passes through my body and I look compulsively out the window. All I see is a pane spattered with droplets of water and beyond, a cloudy sky. "Where are we? What floor are we on?" I ask urgently.

Carlos tilts his head, confused, which makes two of us, because I don't know what I'm so worried about. "Harborview Medical Center. Eighth floor."

I rake my fingers through my hair. "I think that's okay." I fall quiet for a moment and stare out the windowpane. "Did I say anything else when I was sick?"

"You asked for your dad a bunch of times."

"So I have a family."

"Sounds like it. At least a dad. Maybe he's back in Colombia?"

I nod, but my forehead wrinkles. "I feel like maybe, but there's something... I guess I don't know for sure."

Carlos takes his hand off mine and laces his fingers together on top of the thin bedspread. "They wouldn't tell me much about you, about what was going on. I mean, I overheard them talking about the infection and the blood poisoning and stuff because I've been in the room, and when you started responding to the antibiotics, they told me you were going to be okay, but they know I'm not your family, so they wouldn't give me much detail about anything."

"How do they know who my family is or isn't? I don't even know." The reality of that statement hits me, and I lean back on my pillow and stare out the window. A smattering of raindrops hit the glass and I flinch.

"I was so worried you were going to die on me, I wasn't

thinking straight. I told the ER nurse your name was Lita, but that I didn't know your last name. I should have just made something up. But I didn't. That might have sailed right over a doctor's head, but nurses are pretty sharp." Carlos rubs the bedspread nervously between his thumb and index finger. "When you changed into that dress and I saw your port, I knew you were really sick. I recognized it from when my mom had cancer. It made me wonder" – Carlos ducks his head and his voice drops – "if you do too."

I sit up and hug my knees to my chest. "I don't know. Maybe."

Carlos stares firmly at the ground.

"I didn't remember that port, and I don't know how it got there. I saw it for the first time when I changed my clothes in the bathroom at that store, what was it called?"

"Goodwill."

"Right. I saw the port in the mirror there. I didn't know what it was for, but it looked really gross."

Carlos sniffs, rubs his eyes, and looks up at me again. "My mom had one. It's how she got her chemo for the last year before she died. It never looked like yours, though."

I unwrap my arms from around my legs and take Carlos's hand. "I'm so sorry about your mom. How old were you?"

"Eleven."

My throat clogs with emotion. "I lost someone I loved when I was eleven." My eyes pop wide open, and I wrack my brain, trying to pull on that thread, but there's nothing there. The little wisp of memory has fizzled out and coiled back down into my brain stem.

"Who was it?" Carlos asks.

I shake my head and squeeze my eyes shut. "I don't remember."

There's a tap on the door and a redhead with glasses pokes her head in. "Time for vitals... How about that! You're awake." She scowls at Carlos. "You should have hit the call light." She strides into the room. "Excuse me," she says to Carlos. There's a bit of an edge to her voice, and I can't tell if she's irritated with him specifically, or just stressed.

"My name is Nancy, and I'll be your nurse for" – she glances at her wrist – "about an hour. Fifty-three minutes to shift change. God, I wish you could have waited until after report to wake up."

"Want me to pretend to go back to sleep?" I ask.

Nancy sighs and smiles distractedly, one eye on her clipboard and one on me. "No, I can't do that. Hippocratic oath and all that." She pulls something out of her pocket and drags it across my forehead. It beeps rapidly, ending in one long sustained bleat. "Ninety-nine point four. Much, much better." She slips a cuff around my arm and flicks something to make it inflate until it's squeezing almost hard enough to be unpleasant, then it deflates. "One thirty-five over eighty-five. Better than it was, but we should check your kidneys. I'll have the doc write an order for an ultrasound. Let's check your surgical site. Sir?" She angles her head at Carlos.

He stands up. "I know the drill." He pushes his chair back into the corner of the room. "I have to leave for this part," he says. "I didn't want you to be alone when you woke up. Now that you're awake, I'm gonna run down the hill and check on my tent. I won't be gone long." Carlos grabs his backpack from under the chair and leaves me alone with the nurse.

"Let's take a look then." Nancy unties the front of my hospital gown and opens it, exposing me from the waist up. I have a large white square on my chest, held down with tape around all four edges. "Dressing looks good," she murmurs. She peels a corner of the tape and lifts the bandage up. "Wow, well done," she says.

I stare at the spot in my chest where the port used to be. It's gone. The red lines and swelling are gone as well. My skin has been pulled shut around where the hole was and sewn together with black thread. I move as though to touch the spot with my finger, but Nancy grabs my hand and guides it away.

"Hey, no touching. You're not going to derail your miraculous recovery on my watch. Save it for night shift."

I don't know why, but I'm filled with a sense of loss, mixed with dread. "Where did it go?"

"Straight into the incinerator, I hope. That thing just about killed you, sweetie."

I blink back tears.

Nancy writes a few things on a sheet of paper on her clipboard, slides it into a plastic pocket on the wall, turns back to me, and notices my wet eyes. "I imagine your life isn't easy," she says, more gently than she's spoken to me before.

I shrug halfheartedly. I imagine it isn't either.

"Your friend seems nice. Barely left your side. Have you been with him long?"

I know the answer to this one. "No. Not long."

"You could do worse, I'm sure."

I don't know if she's complimenting him or criticizing me, so I search around for a way to redirect the conversation. "His mom had cancer. He said she had a port thing like I did."

"Yeah, they're really useful for people who are actually sick." She heaves her heaviest sigh so far and crosses her arms over her chest. "Sweetie, I'm not a social worker, but I feel like I have to give you some advice. You're still young. We ran a full STD panel. Somehow, you've dodged every bullet out there. You're clean. Once this infection completely clears your system, you're going to be quite healthy, if on the small side. So please, I'm begging you, *please* do not do this again. I don't know what street MD you went to for that port, but it's too dangerous. You have your whole life ahead of you, and if you make the right choices, it can be a good one. There are services and programs to help you."

I blink at her rapidly. I've understood almost none of what she's said. "Um, okay?" I respond, but it comes out way more like a question than I meant it to.

Nancy sighs. "Listen, I have to go give report. Your night

nurse is Becky, and she has a real big issue with IV drug users taking up beds in the med/surg unit. I'd keep your finger off your call light, if you know what I mean."

"Don't ask her for help," I translate.

"Remember how you told me when I came in that you could pretend to be asleep?"

I nod. "Yeah."

"Do that for Becky. Just don't tell her."

---

I spend the next hour watching the television in the upper corner of my room, delighted by the images that flicker across it. It seems to be the story of a family that lives in two rooms in a small tower. They get along much better than I'd expect them to, existing in such close quarters.

I'm so drawn in, I don't even notice the person standing in my doorway until she taps on the frame. "Housekeeping," she announces.

I straighten up sharply in bed. She pushes a cart into the room. Her hair is slicked back into a tight bun at the nape of her neck and she moves rapidly, dumping the contents of a small square receptacle into a larger bin. She grabs the empty tray from where Carlos had been sitting and slides it into her cart, then turns to me with a smile. "If you're still hungry, I can get you a yogurt or a cheese stick from the kitchen in the unit."

At the mention of food, my stomach gurgles a bit. I don't tell her that I wasn't the one who ate from the tray. I don't know if it would get Carlos in trouble or not. "That sounds wonderful, thank you."

A different voice snaps from the doorway. "This isn't the Hilton."

The housekeeper and I both shoot our gazes to the door, where a tall blonde woman stands with a distasteful expression on her face. I instantly dislike her, and I'm certain the feeling is mutual.

The housekeeper smiles again, but it seems strained and apologetic rather than friendly this time, and she leaves without saying another word.

"So, the sleeper awakes, huh?" the nurse says, flouncing into the room.

"You must be Becky," I answer.

"Yes, and you're Lita, last name unknown. Care to enlighten me, and I'll update your chart?"

My eyes flick to the screen in the corner where the short, dark-haired man is giving some sort of monologue. "Hofstadter," I say firmly.

The nurse's eyes follow mine to the screen. "Lita Hofstadter. Right. I'll let you think on that a little more."

"That's my name," I say stubbornly. "Take it or leave it."

I know I shouldn't pick a fight with this person – she's clearly in a position of power over me – but I can't stand her, with her smooth skin and blonde hair and superciliously arched eyebrows. Another image flashes across my mind, a similar face, a sneer. I feel like the bed has been snatched from under me and I gasp at the falling sensation. My hands fly to my sides, pressing into the firm, very real mattress beneath me.

"Your blood pressure spiked. We need to get that kidney ultrasound scheduled. And you probably need a tetanus booster."

My heart hammers. "I need a thousand of them," I blurt.

The nurse snorts. "Yeah, I bet you do." She pulls the clipboard out of the wall pocket, jots something down on it, and replaces it with a clatter. "Listen, I'm going to take care of you because that's my job, but I want you to know that you're taking valuable bed space from someone who actually needs it. We should be able send you home as an outpatient with an IV drip, but we know you'd be slamming dope within the hour, so we keep you admitted where you're waited on hand and foot and fed for free three times a day. How fair is that to the elderly woman with the UTI still waiting in the ER for a bed?" She scowls and answers her own question. "Not fair at all."

I can't let this woman stand here hurling accusations at me. Being blamed unfairly like this is creepily familiar, but the memory is so slippery, I can't grab on to the feelings roiling around inside me and follow their threads back to images that make any sense. I know she's wrong about me, though. "I don't think I'm who you say I am."

"Oh yeah? It's been two days and your toxicology report still isn't back from the lab. Your blood sample probably broke the centrifuge." She leans over me, her eyes inches from mine. "When you're discharged, I fully expect it to be in handcuffs."

"And if you keep talking to her that way, I fully expect you to lose your license." Carlos strides into the room, followed by Dez.

Carlos positions himself by my bedside, his stance firm. "Her IV fluids should be discontinued, her antibiotics need to be re-hung, and her catheter should be removed as soon as possible. And yet you stand here berating her instead. And what about that kidney ultrasound? Are you going to get it ordered or not?" He and the nurse stare at each other without blinking.

She breaks first. "I have other patients. This isn't a homeless shelter. Keep your visit short."

Carlos nods but doesn't speak. Dez sinks into the chair in the corner, not looking at all ready to go anywhere. The nurse spins on her heel and stalks out. She flings the door closed behind her, but it doesn't slam; a cushion of air makes it close with a soft click.

"How did you know what to say to her?" I ask.

"I spent a lot of time in hospitals when my mom was sick. I wasn't homeless back then; people treated me differently. I know the lingo."

"Thank you. She seemed to know more about me than I do. Or at least she thought she did."

"Yeah, believe me, I get it."

In the corner, Dez sighs heavily. "So, you going to tell her?"

I blink and my gaze shifts between the two of them. "Tell me what?"

Carlos grimaces, but it's Dez who speaks. "The tent, our stuff... It's all gone, man. While Carlos was up here watching you sleep, the cops came and tore down the tent. Wiped it all out."

"Oh my god, I'm so sorry."

"It wasn't your fault," Carlos says to me. "It would have still happened whether I'd been there with Dez or not."

"You don't know that," Dez says darkly. "You're fast on your feet. Maybe you could have talked them out of it."

"And maybe we would have both gotten arrested," Carlos shoots back. "That's the thing. You never know what might have happened – you only know where you are. And yeah, it's crap, but we're alive and we're free and we've gotta build from there."

"God, you're such an optimist." Dez moans. "I'm number nine thousand and one on the transitional housing list," he chirps, tipping his head side to side. "Just gotta keep making those weekly phone calls and I'll be in a house in no time." He snorts. "I used to think the whole glass half-full thing was cool, but dude, it's just too much right now."

I have no idea what Dez is talking about; he may as well be speaking a foreign language.

Carlos opens his mouth to say something in response but reconsiders and presses his lips shut into a thin line.

Dez sits for a few more moments in silence, then shakes his head and puts his hands on his knees, pushing himself to standing. "I don't wanna do this anymore. It was a cool experiment, but we lost. I'm gonna move back to The Jungle. Safety in numbers. They won't mess with us there."

Carlos's face falls. "Dude, no. You know what it's like in there. Come on, it's not worth it. We can stay here until Lita gets better.

Three meals a day, and a free shower down the hall. After that, it's summer. We'll get out of the city. Take the train north."

Dez shakes his head. "No way. You heard that nurse. 'This isn't a homeless shelter,'" he mimics. "We can't stay here."

Carlos waves his hand toward the door. "That nurse'll be gone at shift change. We cycle out often enough, hang in the cafeteria for an hour, whatever, no one will know we're living here."

My eyes dart back and forth between Carlos and Dez. Dez locks eyes with me, then breaks our gaze. "If it was just us, I'd say yeah. But I don't want to be a tripod."

Carlos's eyes widen and his nostrils flare. "Lita can pick any lock you throw in front of her. I've seen her do it. We'd never go hungry again. Plus, dude, she's sick. She has no one."

Dez's face twists. "She has Jimmy."

"Yeah, well, where is he? I don't see him banging down the door to collect her."

"Fine, you stay here, and I'll go to The Jungle and tell Jimmy where she's at. That'll get me in good for sure, and it'll get her taken care of. After that, we can decide what to do long term. Win, win."

Carlos turns to stare at me, then jerks his head toward the door. "Come on. Let's talk about it in the hall."

Dez walks out without saying goodbye, but from the look on his face, I'm certain he's not coming back. I hear muffled voices as Carlos closes the door behind me, then nothing. I sit quietly for a long time. On the television, the people talk to each other, laugh, make faces, and stride in and out of each other's quarters. I keep the sound muted. Finally, the door clicks and I sag with relief, but it's just my nurse, Becky, again.

She strides into the room and takes an aggressive stance with her left hip cocked. "Righthanded or left?" she asks without preamble.

Is there any end to easy questions that I don't have the answer to? I think back to picking the lock for Carlos. I spun the dial with my right hand. "Righthanded."

"Gimme your left arm."

I extend my arm toward her. She grabs it and twists, swipes my arm with something wet, then jabs me with a needle I didn't realize she had in her hand.

"Ow!" I try not to jerk away while the needle remains in my tricep. As soon as she withdraws it, I yank my arm back. "What did you do that for?" I ask, rubbing the sore spot.

"Tetanus booster. If you're going to be transferred into police custody, it's easier to have this sort of thing taken care of before your arrest," she says airily.

I swallow a huge lump in my throat. "What do you mean?"

She smiles. "Your toxicology report just came back."

I wait several moments for her to continue, but she just stands there grinning at me. "Well?" I finally ask. "What did it say?"

Becky tosses her head and slips the needle she just poked me with into a container on the wall labeled 'biohazard.' "I haven't read it yet." She sneers. "The file's a hundred and ten kilobytes, so I put a pot of coffee on."

There's a tap on the door, and a man pokes his head in. "Radiology transport."

"That was fast," Becky says.

"Slow night," the man says, entering the room. He has dark skin and kind eyes, and I instantly feel better with him in the room.

"My name's Bereket," he says in a sonorous voice. "I'll be taking you downstairs for your ultrasound." He turns to Becky. "Is she ambulatory? Her record didn't specify."

Becky shrugs. "We don't know. She just woke up a couple hours ago."

Bereket raises his eyebrow, and I can tell he's not thrilled with her answer. "Come," he says to me with a smile. "You're light. I'm sure you fly like a ballerina, but let's see if you walk like a young lady."

Becky rolls her eyes, but Bereket ignores her and helps me off the bed. He makes sure I'm stable, then shows me how to hold the pole my IV is connected to and roll it with me as I take my first steps in days. I'm apparently a little too wobbly for his tastes because he makes me get into the wheelchair he has by the door. "We'll do some more walking when we get back, I promise," he says as he wheels me down the hallway.

We stop at a pair of double metal doors set into a recess in the wall, and my heart pounds. A panicked whimpering sound worms its way out of my throat.

"Don't like elevators, huh?" Bereket says. "I understand. My wife doesn't, either, while I dislike escalators. It makes it very difficult to shop in the mall." Before I know it, the doors have opened and he's whisked me inside. "I promise nothing bad will happen to you on my watch," he says, and he keeps up a running stream of commentary, which keeps my panic at bay until finally the doors slide open again.

"Thank you," I choke out when he's pushed me over the threshold and back into a tiled hallway. "I don't know why that scared me so much."

"Some fears cannot be explained," Bereket says kindly.

"I can't explain a lot of things right now," I mumble.

He wheels me down a long hallway until we reach a door marked 'Radiology,' which he opens and pushes me through. "I'll get you checked in," Bereket says. He reaches to his hip, pulls a square off his belt, and holds it up to examine it. "Odd, your nurse just paged me. Perhaps they're adding something to your order. I'll be right back."

Before Bereket can take more than a step away, however, the double doors at the end of the room burst open and a herd of people in papery suits barge through. "We found them," one of them barks into a cell phone. Then he turns laser focus to us.

"The ultrasound is canceled. There's nothing wrong with her kidneys," he says.

"That's fine," Bereket says slowly. "I can take her back to her room."

"No," the man replies. "She's being transferred to the decontamination suite. And Mr. Kidane? You're going to need to come with us too."

# CHAPTER NINE

June 23, 2018

Bereket and a small army of people race me through a maze of corridors, then into an elevator. Nobody says a word. Bereket's eyes are as wide and confused as I'm sure mine must be. I want to jump from the wheelchair and take off running, but I know I can't. I could barely toddle across my room just a few minutes earlier, and I'm still hooked to an IV, which one of the paper-suited minions drags rapidly alongside us as we charge through the hospital.

Bereket and I are pushed into separate rooms. I'm stripped of my hospital gown, and it's stuffed into a large container marked 'biohazard' like the one in my previous room, but bigger. A paper-suited person unceremoniously slides the IV out of my hand, then guides me into a shower stall and I don't even have time to be embarrassed that they're seeing me naked before water blasts me from all directions. I'm dizzy, and my legs feel weak. I sink to the floor and wrap my arms around my knees.

When they've decided I'm wet enough, the water shuts off and someone in a paper suit scrubs me all over with soap and a soft cloth, then I'm hosed down again. I don't talk, and neither does my handler. I almost feel like I'm outside my body observing the whole thing at this point.

Finally, I must be clean enough because the water turns off for good, and the paper-suited person helps me stand, towels me off, then holds out a fresh hospital gown. "Arms out," a female voice says firmly but not unkindly. It's the first thing she's said to me this entire time.

Obediently, I thrust my arms into the short sleeves of the gown and she ties it in the back, then supports me as she guides me through a doorway and over to a bed.

There, she reinserts a new IV. It's a little uncomfortable going in – the skin on my hand feels thin and abused – but it doesn't take her long and she seems happy with her work. When she straightens the needle and tapes it down, the ache goes away almost instantly.

"Try to relax," she says. "The doctor will be in in a moment."

Try to relax? Is she delusional? I have little time to ponder that thought, however, because almost as soon as she's stepped out, a man in a similar but different colored paper suit comes in.

He looks me up and down. "So, you're the young lady who has this place in quite an uproar."

I lift my chin, but I have no reply for him.

"I'm Doctor Blank. I'll be taking over your case. We've recalled all the staff members who've worked with you, and we're following decon protocols with them as well."

"Everyone's getting a surprise shower?"

The doctor nods.

"Becky must be thrilled."

The doctor snorts behind his paper mask, fogging up his eye shield a bit. He waits for it to clear, and he has himself under control by the time it does. "She's not your biggest fan."

I don't argue.

"I know you only woke recently, and I understand you didn't have a close connection with your nursing staff."

"I liked the first nurse," I say.

Despite how nice and reasonable he seems, I'm certain this guy couldn't care less who I did and didn't like. He's looking for answers. "You've indicated you're from Colombia."

"That's right." I cling to one of the very few things I'm absolutely certain of. I won't let him take that away from me. But he tries.

"Your accent is intriguing, but I can't place it. However...it doesn't sound South American to me." He taps his gloved fingers together. "More likely Ukrainian, or possibly East Asian?" He leans forward. "What I want to know is, where did you come from? By way of Chernobyl perhaps? Or Fukushima? And how did you get here?"

I shake my head. "I'm from Columbia. I know that for sure."

The doctor sighs. "That's difficult for me to believe, but I suppose I'll have to – for now. Though I can assure you if the CDC decides to investigate your situation, they will probably not simply take you at your word."

I can't give him anything else. I decide to lay my cards on the table. This guy isn't my friend, but for some reason, I trust him. He's not out to get me. Not like Becky was. "I don't know what happened to me," I say quietly. "I don't have any memories before just a couple of days ago. I don't even remember my name." I swallow. "But I know I'm from Columbia. I'm righthanded. I'm scared of elevators. And... And..." I scrabble around for something else to say, a fact about myself that I'm sure of. "And I can pick locks. But I don't know why."

"The boys who brought you to the ER in the first place. What were their names?"

Instantly my guard flies up. "I don't remember," I lie. "Just some random guys I met on the street."

The doctor raises his eyebrows behind his mask. "I understand one of those 'random guys' didn't leave your side until you woke up a few hours ago."

"He's homeless," I say, plucking the word that Becky used to describe him. "He had nowhere else to go."

"Mm-hmm." The doctor murmurs, but I know he's not convinced. "I'd like to get them back here and admit them for decontamination as well. We don't need a radiation exposure issue trickling through our homeless community."

I tilt my head and furrow my brow. "What do you mean?"

The doctor puts his gloved hand on top of my hand, the one without the IV poking into it. "I mean that your toxicology report came back clean. You're not a drug addict, or if you are, you've been sober for quite some time. There were unidentifiable compounds in your sample, but I believe that's due to the fact that you have enough nuclear material in your bloodstream to power a small city."

My mouth drops open.

"And everyone you've come in contact with is at mild to moderate risk of contamination themselves. We're taking no chances."

The doctor stares intently into my eyes. "This news doesn't jog your memory?"

I look down and shake my head.

"It's why I asked you about Chernobyl and Fukushima. Those are the biggest radiological disaster sites on our Western radar. Neither of those ring a bell?"

I keep my eyes downcast and shrug. "No. I'm sorry."

"Eastern Washington?" the doctor says hopefully. "Hanford?"

I look at him again. "Nope. Nothing. I really am sorry. I wish I could help you."

He sighs. "I wish you could too." He claps his hands together. "But despite the fact that you can't seem to give me what I want, I'm still going to help you. I'm going to put you on potassium iodide and Prussian Blue. I've already got you on a DTPA drip."

He waves his hand at the IV bag hanging from the metal stand. "We'll see how you respond to that, and I'm also prescribing two weeks of Neupogen injections. We're going to try to take your radioactivity level from weapons-grade to that of a delicious microwaved pizza. You do remember what a microwave pizza is, don't you?"

Whatever makes him feel better. "Sure. Of course I do."

# CHAPTER TEN

July 1, 2018

Doctor Blank says I've improved tremendously. He says I'm not 'shedding isotopes' anymore, whatever that means, and he gets me transferred to a new room. This one, thank god, has a television. For the last week, other than Doctor Blank and the occasional tight-lipped nurse, my only companionship has been the beeping machines I'm hooked to.

I can't wait to catch up on the antics of Leonard, Sheldon, and the other people in their quarters. I wonder what they've been up to. But the remote is just barely in my hand before two men in suits arrive. One is tall and powerfully built. The other is slender, with eyebrows that meet in the middle. They don't introduce themselves the way all of my nurses have. They just stand by my bedside, notebooks in hand, and fire question after question at me in hard, cold voices.

"Where are you from? How did you get here? Are you in the country legally? What were the chemicals in your bloodstream?"

Forty-five minutes later, they're still harassing me and writing in their little notebooks, and I can't stop darting glances at the remote control on my bedside table. I'd much rather be watching the people on the television. This is both boring and annoying. Their questions are total repeats of the ones Doctor Blank has asked me, but they're not being even slightly nice about it, and no matter how many times I tell them I don't remember the answers to their questions, they act like I'm lying.

I almost wish I could just tell them what they want to know so that they'll leave me alone, but I can't say where I was exposed to radiation, where I came from, who my parents are, or what the unidentified chemicals in my bloodstream were, because I don't know.

One of the men instructs a nurse to take a new vial of blood from me for testing, and I feel smug. I know my blood will keep my secrets because it's clean now. Doctor Blank had me on a ton of different medicines over the last week, and he told me before he moved me to my new room that the unidentified chemicals are gone. The doctor said something about a half life, and I thought he was talking about the chemicals, but he could just as easily be talking about my existence because that's what it feels like to me in this boring hospital.

The man with the intersecting eyebrows looks up from his notepad and finally asks me something different. "The boys who brought you to the hospital. I understand they stayed with you for some time. Who were they?"

My heart pounds painfully. Only one of the boys had stayed with me. I never expected to see Dez again when he left my hospital room a week ago. It's not thoughts of him that have been keeping me up at night. I close my eyes and picture warm brown eyes and a crooked smile. I really thought Carlos would return. I felt like I'd meant something to him. Like I'd mattered. But as the long days and interminable nights ticked by, I had to face reality. Carlos isn't coming back.

"Hey," the eyebrow guy barks. I hear a snapping sound and my eyes fly open. His fingers are right in front of my face. "Pay attention when I'm talking to you."

Anger surges through my body and I want to break his offensive fingers *snap, snap, snap* before he even knows what I'm doing. But I ball my fists at my sides and force myself to take slow, controlled breaths. They don't know how strong I've gotten. I'm not going to give away any of my advantage now.

"I don't know their names. They were just some homeless kids whose tent I fell into. They were only here for the free food." It's the first time I've lied to these guys, and I feel great about it.

Eyebrow frowns and exchanges sighs with his partner. He jots something else on his notepad.

The nurse draws my blood, and she doesn't say anything, but she has a sympathetic look on her face. She can't stand up to these guys, either, whoever they are. I feel for her, but she's not in their crosshairs like I am, so I feel a lot worse for myself.

Even though Carlos is gone from my life, I'm proud of myself for keeping him anonymous this whole time. I never once mentioned his name to Doctor Blank or any of my nurses. Carlos helped me when I had no one, and for that I'm in his debt. I might have asked about him. I might have said something to Doctor Blank or one of my nurses. *Have you seen him? Has he stopped by at all to check on me?* But I stayed silent. Because even though I'd grown to trust Doctor Blank over this last week in the hospital, I've never had anything but suspicion for the camera mounted in the corner of my room. I have the distinct feeling I'm being watched day and night, through that cold, clear lens, and if I owed Carlos anything at all, it was privacy.

The men finally appear to have grown sick of me, because they flip their notebooks shut, tell me they'll see me again soon, and leave. Huffing irritably, I grab the remote control for the television and my thumb is on the power button when Doctor Blank walks in the door.

I heave a huge, theatrical sigh.

Doctor Blank totally ignores it and greets me in his typical fashion. "How are you feeling today? Thumbs up, thumbs down, or thumbs sideways?"

I curl my fingers into a ball and stick my thumb out parallel to the floor. I'm always 'thumbs sideways' for Doctor Blank.

"I understand you had visitors."

"Yeah. They were jerks."

Doctor Blank's naturally droopy eyes turn down a little more at the corners, and he glances at one of my beeping monitors. "I think it's about time we got you in for that kidney ultrasound," he says, tapping the business end of his pen against my chart. "I have some concerns about your blood pressure. It tends to spike when I enter the room."

"Do you ever think maybe it's you?"

Doctor Blank gives me a perturbed look.

I shrug. "I never know what you're going to say to me. Is my blood radioactive? Has it turned purple? Did I die, and you're just now coming to tell me? It's stressful."

Doctor Blank chuckles. "You're a very changed young woman from when I met you a week ago. And not just because you've lost your green undertones and you've grown two centimeters." He pats me on the knee. "Maybe I do stress you out. But I still want to rule out kidney issues. Besides, you should be delighted. An ultrasound means you get to leave this room, even if it is for only a little while."

"Oh, wow, a different hospital room for yet another test. I can't wait."

"It's still a step in the right direction. Take what you can get."

"I know," I mutter. "I just wish..."

"What?"

I stare at the corner of the room, the one away from the camera. "I don't know. I wish somebody cared."

"I care."

"You're my doctor. It's a job requirement."

There's a tap at the door. "Radiology transport."

I'm disappointed. I'd been hoping I would see Bereket again, but this is a female voice. Doctor Blank's right, though. I should be happy about getting out of the room. I paste a look on my face that might be a smile, but which is probably a grimace. I think about pushing myself to standing but decide against it. I let the woman from transport come around to my side of the bed, and she and Doctor Blank help me into the wheelchair.

Doctor Blank lingers in the doorway. "You'll have more visitors this afternoon, so I don't know when I'll have a chance to discuss your kidney results with you."

"More visitors like the guys in suits?"

He nods, and I roll my eyes. "I'm not going to be able to tell them anything that I couldn't tell the other guys."

Doctor Blank swallows. "It's been a real pleasure helping you get better, Lita. Thank you."

"Um...you're welcome?"

The doctor laughs, but it doesn't reach his eyes. He squeezes the door frame. "Let's get a look at those rock star kidneys."

I curl my fingers into a ball and hold my thumb sideways, then stick it up to a ten-degree angle.

"Thanks." Doctor Blank says. "I'll take it."

---

The lady from transport wheels me silently through the hospital. I know I should be thrilled to get out of the room, but there's little to be enthusiastic about in the deserted, echoey hallways.

A tall janitor pushes a mop at a spot on the floor with an excitement level that matches the beige colored walls. He lifts the mop into his bucket, swishes it around, then leans down to wring its floppy gray strands out as we pass, the muscles on his right arm standing out as he works the lever, his face hidden by a mask.

*That's an N95 respirator*, I think to myself, but I barely have time to wonder where that thought came from before we turn a corner and a set of wooden double doors marked 'Radiology' stands in front of us. The transport woman slaps a silver square on the wall and the doors open with a hum.

A woman with a round face and curly reddish hair looks up from behind a desk. "Whatcha got for me?"

"Blood pressure spikes. Rule out kidney issues," my transporter says.

"When do you get those pressure spikes, sweetie?" the receptionist asks.

"Whenever the doctor comes into my room."

She chuckles. "Idiots. Your kidneys are fine. But we'll wand you and get it on record. Have you ever had an ultrasound before?"

"I don't think so."

"Well, they're nothing to worry about. Just a little cold when the gel goes on." She taps a few buttons on her keyboard and nods at my transport. "Okay, she's all set in the system."

The transporter positions my wheelchair in a small waiting area. "Where to next?" she asks the receptionist.

"I don't have anything else for you right now; the census is pretty light."

The transporter tightens her ponytail. "Do you mind if I take my lunch then?"

The receptionist shrugs one shoulder. "It's as good a time as any. This one" – she smiles at me kindly, so I know she's not belittling me – "ought to take about twenty minutes. I'll page you when she's ready to return to her floor, but make sure you take your full lunch. You don't mind if you have to wait a bit for transport, do you, sweetie?"

It appears I'll never get to watch television like I want to, but what am I supposed to say? I shake my head. "It's fine with me."

"Thanks." The transport woman smiles her goodbye, presses a

silver square on this side of the doors, and walks through once they've opened.

"Oh, hey," the receptionist calls, but it's not the transport lady she's speaking to. Her voice has changed – it's higher-pitched and flirty. "Do you have time to make your way in here? Dayshift cooked fish in the microwave and I'm about to keel over from the smell."

A voice from the corridor replies. "I'm yours anytime you need me, Anna."

The hair on my arms stands straight up.

"Oh, Steven, you are the best. I'm putting you in for employee of the month. Don't think I won't."

The tall janitor we passed in the hallway walks in, his brown eyes trained on Anna, his face hidden behind the paper hospital mask that loops behind each ear. "Employee of the month?" he says in a joking voice muffled by his mask. "I'm too new." My portable heart rate monitor emits a peal as my pulse accelerates.

"Keep up the way you're going and you'll be running this place," Anna says with a toothy grin.

The janitor walks behind the desk and down an angled hallway without looking at me once.

A tech steps around the corner with a clipboard in his hand. "Lita Hofstadter?" he says, raising his eyebrows.

I glance around the lobby, devoid of all people except me, and I jump a bit in my seat. "Oh, yeah," I say. I'm still unfamiliar with my hastily made up last name. And my first name, for that matter.

The tech circles behind me, grabs the handles of my wheel-chair, and maneuvers me down the hall that shoots off the opposite angle from the way the janitor went. I crane my neck, hoping to catch one last glimpse of him. *I'd thought for a second…but no.*

The tech pushes me into a room and swings the door shut behind us.

"My name's Dave. I'll be doing your ultrasound. How mobile are you?"

"Well, I came here in a wheelchair. You tell me."

Dave rolls his eyes. "That's no indication. Everyone's on wheels in this place. Keeps the transport guys employed."

I glance at the corners of the room. Spying no cameras, I shrug. "I'm all right."

"I see you play your cards close to the vest," Dave says, and a mental image of the silver vest I was wearing when I first met Carlos flashes through my mind. I feel a searing sense of loss. That janitor reminded me so much of Carlos. For an instant I miss him so much I can almost taste it, bitter, like copper shavings in my mouth. But Carlos is gone, along with that vest and everything else I arrived here with. I breathe deeply and try to drain my mind of the thoughts that flood it like filthy churning water.

Dave doesn't seem to notice my mental turmoil. "I don't blame ya. It's easy to develop trust issues in this place. Hop yourself on up on that table then, and let's get your kidneys under the wand."

I jerk myself to a standing position, lean on the edge of the table, then swing my legs up and around so that they stick straight out on front of me. It feels so good to move my body without unnecessary help. The tightness in my chest loosens and my next deep breath doesn't feel so forced.

"Great job," the tech says. "I'm going to adjust the table and get this show on the road. We'll be done here in no time."

I lie on the table and try not to squirm when the tech smears jelly on my torso and rubs a wand all over me. I count seconds to keep my mind occupied and prevent it from slipping back to a dark place of loss and longing. I've counted to nine hundred and twelve when Dave puts his wand away. He dusts his hands together. "We have to wait for the radiologist's report for it to be official, but your kidneys look fine to me." He wipes the jelly off my body with a soft cloth. "You're all done. Mount your trusty steed and I'll gallop you back to the lobby."

I'm pretty sure he means 'get in the wheelchair,' so I scoot off the table, straighten out my hospital gown, and reluctantly climb aboard. I'd rather walk, but even more than that, I'd rather not argue with anyone, so I just do as I'm told.

"She's all set," the tech tells the receptionist. The janitor called her "Anna," I remember. Anna holds a finger in the air while she cradles a phone to her ear and nods, like the person on the other end can see her. I sit alone in the sterile lobby. There's nothing for me to do, and I'm sick and tired of counting, so I memorize a fire evacuation route diagram for about one thousand years. Anna finally hangs up the phone, then picks it right back up and punches a few buttons. "I'll page transport for you."

I flash her a 'thumbs sideways,' and she knits her eyebrows at me. Maybe that only works on doctors. After what feels like forever, Anna makes a snorting noise. "Hmpf." She frowns at her telephone, references her computer screen, then looks back at her phone. She picks up the phone and punches at the keypad, then sets it back in its cradle. She looks over at me. "Transport's not answering the page."

She frowns, stands up, and puts her hand on her abdomen. "I don't have anybody scheduled for the next thirty minutes, I'm starving, I need a cigarette, and they're not answering. Figures."

The janitor lopes around the corner. "I got that microwave cleaned out for you, but the smell was still there, so I took everything out of the fridge and bleached it to within an inch of its life. Problem solved."

Anna dimples at him. "You're the best. The. Best."

"I overheard you can't get a hold of transport. I can push her back to wherever she goes so you can take your break. She doesn't look too complicated."

"Oh, would you?" Anna slaps her palms on her desktop. "She's got an IV pole and a pulse oximeter, so we honestly don't need a real transporter, just someone to push the chair to the right place."

The janitor spares a look at me. "What do you think? Okay if I push you around?"

My breath catches in a giant bubble in my throat as Carlos's brown eyes lock on to mine. I swallow hard. "That's fine with me."

---

Neither of us says a word as Carlos wheels me briskly down the hallway and into a waiting elevator. As soon as the doors slide shut, Carlos rips off his mask and presses his finger on the 'B' button. He reaches into his pocket and pulls out a pager. "I liberated this from the transporter after she dropped you off."

My eyes widen and I say the first thing that pops into my head. "I thought you didn't steal."

Carlos steps in front of my wheelchair and crouches so we're eye to eye. "I don't usually. But I know how to when it's important." He places his hands over mine. "Here's the deal. We don't have much time. We've got one shot to bust you out of here, and it's right now. So you've got to decide. Are you with me?"

"Bust me out? It's boring and yeah, I don't like it here, but why would I do that? They're taking care of me."

Carlos's lip curls. "Your doctor is a legit guy, and he's protected you as much as he can. But you're healthy now. Healthy enough for them to arrest you."

My breath catches in my throat, and Carlos continues. "Remember the people the doctor warned you about, the ones waiting in your room when you get back?"

I shake my head. "It didn't seem like a warning." The elevator bumps to a soft stop and the doors open. Carlos pushes me out into an empty hallway and parks me in a recessed area with men's and women's restrooms on either side and a water fountain in the middle. He kneels in front of me again.

"I was outside your room listening. You can stick your head in the sand all you want, but people from the sheriff's office don't just stop by and visit everyone. I pulled up your medical records one night when no one was looking. You had drugs in your system they can't even identify. Detectives from the sheriff's office are waiting for you right now, and they'll arrest you the instant you get back to your room."

"What?" I feel my eyes grow big in my head. "What's a sheriff? I thought those guys were just notepad people."

Carlos's eyes grow as wide as mine must be. "Seriously, Lita? A sheriff is a cop. They're going to take you to juvie."

I stop breathing. "I can't go to juvie. I'll drown in juvie."

Carlos nods curtly. "Yeah, most people do. So you can leave right now, with me, or you can go back to your room and leave in handcuffs. Your choice."

I stare into his eyes, trying to see all the way through and into his brain, as if his thoughts would be written there for me to read. But they're not, and all I see are his earnest, intelligent brown eyes and the tension knotting his forehead. "I'm with you."

Carlos lets out a breath. "Okay. We've already wasted too much time. I've got to pull your IV. It might hurt a little bit coming out."

I squeeze my eyes shut tight. "Do it."

I feel pressure and a slight pain in my hand, and I look down. The IV is gone. "Wow. It hurt more when the nurse did it the last time."

"Maybe next time I'll pretend to be a nurse instead of a janitor."

"You don't work here?"

Carlos scoffs and flips his ID badge. "Steven Sylvester will never get paid for all the overtime he's been pulling, especially on the radiology floor. When I couldn't lurk in your unit, I hung out there. I knew they'd bring you in for that ultrasound sometime, so I got in good with the staff."

A woman brushes past us and enters the restroom. Carlos frowns at the door as it swings shut, but he shakes it off and turns back to me. "Can you walk?"

"I haven't tried too much, but I feel strong inside," I say softly. "So, yeah, I think so."

"Okay, when they realize you're gone, they'll be looking for a girl in a wheelchair – a patient. So we need to switch places. You're walking out and pushing me." Carlos reaches into a plastic bag and pulls out the slippery red dress. "I saved this for you."

Inexplicably, my eyes fill with tears and I reach for the fabric.

Carlos points me to the women's room. "Wheel yourself in there since that woman already saw us. I'll take the IV pull and leave it in a stall in the men's room. Change into the dress. I'll meet you right back out here. If anyone else comes into the bathroom, don't act weird. Just try to blend in with the walls."

I'm about to ask him what he means by that, but he gives me a gentle push in the direction of the women's room. "The faster, the better."

I enter and wheel down to the last stall, the large one that accommodates my chair. The other person in the restroom is making all sorts of strange noises, which are creepy but helpful in muffling the sounds I'm making as I untie my hospital gown and stuff it in the chair's back pocket. I slide the dress over my head and it falls just above my knees. The top stretches tight across my breasts. I don't remember it fitting that way before. It's also snugger around the waist. I keep my hospital slippers on; I have no other footwear. I'm not tired at all. I feel a surge of confidence. I'll be able to push Carlos out of here, no problem. The outer restroom door makes a noise as someone pushes it open. I wait for them to go into a stall, but they don't. Carlos said to be quick. Ugh. I'm torn by indecision, but finally I exit the stall and push the wheelchair ahead of me.

A woman stands at the mirror picking at her eye, pulling down her lower lid and rubbing her finger in the pocket below her eyeball. Carlos told me not to be weird. I avert my eyes and walk past her, knowing I'm not going to blend into the beige wall in this silky red dress.

"Aren't you going to wash your hands?" a nasal voice nips.

My gaze flashes to the mirror. The woman massages one eyeball and glares at me with the other.

My brow wrinkles. "I was just changing my clothes." *I don't owe this woman any explanations,* I think. *Why am I defending myself?* I frown and reach to open the door, but the wheelchair is in my way.

The woman gives an exaggerated sigh and slaps the silver square on the side of the wall. The door opens itself with a hum.

Carlos is waiting for me. His eyes widen when he sees me. "Wow. That dress."

"What about it?" I ask defensively.

"Nothing, you just look..." Carlos shifts from foot to foot. "When I first met you, you reminded me of my foster sister, but you don't anymore."

I'm not sure if that's a good thing or a bad thing, but the eye-rubbing woman comes out of the bathroom and scans us up and down suspiciously.

Carlos sinks into the wheelchair. "Thanks, babe. I guess I do still need it," he says.

The woman pulls a rectangle out of her pocket and starts tapping on it. *Cell phone,* my memory supplies unexpectedly. *I've trained on one.*

"Take me upstairs for a smoke, baby," Carlos says in a silky voice that is not his own.

"Okay, moonbeam," I reply.

"Moonbeam?" Carlos mutters as I wheel him away toward the elevators.

"You called me 'baby,' I thought we were doing pet names. Like as part of our disguise."

"Now you're reminding me of my foster sister again. She's the only other person who's ever called me 'moonbeam' and it sounded weird then too."

"It felt right," I hiss, punching the *up* button to call the elevator. I'm so embarrassed and twisted up inside that I don't even remember to be afraid of the elevator when the doors glide open. I just shove him on irritably.

"I like it. I aged out of the foster care system over a year ago, but I was in it for a long time. My foster sister was the only cool thing about state care."

My stomach moves around as the elevator lifts us upward, but only briefly. The doors swish open, and it's a busy floor. People crisscross in every direction, dressed in all sorts of colorful clothing.

Carlos turns his head and speaks out of the side of his mouth. "We've already taken way too long. We gotta get out of here."

"Which way?"

"Left, down the hall, then right at the double glass doors."

The words have no sooner left his mouth than the intercom blares to life in the hallway. "Code Pink, all staff, Code Pink. Please be on the look out for a female teenager in a wheelchair. She is endangered. All staff, Code Pink."

Carlos twists his head around to look at me. "Can you run?" My mouth stretches into what probably looks like a crazy grin, and he nods affirmatively. "Do it." I streak down the hallway, pushing Carlos at top speed. We burst through the double glass doors and out onto the street. "Hang a left," he crows. I turn so sharply, the wheelchair skitters onto its side and dumps my passenger on the sidewalk. He rolls and springs to his feet. "Run!"

Our footsteps hammer the sidewalk, his tread heavier than mine, as I'm still only in paper hospital booties, but my legs pump and I gulp lungfuls of delectable air. I feel like I'm flying and I'm not even scared that I'm going downhill.

"This way." Carlos gasps and darts down a narrow little side street snaking between two tall buildings.

"She's going down the alley!" a man shouts behind us, and I stumble with an overwhelming feeling that this has all happened to me before.

But then Carlos grabs my hand and squeezes. He emits a war cry of exhilarated laughter, and the spell is broken. I join in, and now we're flying, and the shouting male voices fade out as we leave them far behind.

We don't stop running until we reach flat ground, and it takes us even longer to stop laughing. Every time I think I have a grip on myself, my eyes meet Carlos's and I dissolve into giggles again.

Carlos bends at the waist and puts his hands on his knees. I sprawl on my back on a park bench and throw my hands over my eyes, my shoulders shaking with laughter. After a few minutes, I'm finally able to catch my breath, and I sit up, taking notice of the world around me for what feels like the first time.

There are people everywhere, walking on the cobbled streets, coming in and out of doorways. Most clutch packages, but not all. At least half the people peer at cell phones or hold them to their ears. These people are smartly dressed in clean clothes, their hair smooth and shining. Other people are less spiffily put together but seem to have more things. Beady-eyed, feathered creatures strut about, pecking at the street, nibbling at things that I can't see.

Carlos sits down beside me, and we rest in companionable silence. After a minute, I glance over my shoulder. "Do you think they'll keep chasing us?"

Carlos shakes his head. "Nah. Cops have short attention spans, and nobody cares about homeless kids. If they'd caught you back there, you'd be on your way to juvie for sure, but nobody's going to lose any sleep hunting you down. They've got you pegged as a drug addict. I'm sure they figure they'll have another opportunity to arrest you soon."

"No, they won't."

Carlos cocks his head. "I believe you. You were sick when we met, but not dope sick. I don't know what happened to you, but I don't think it was drugs."

"What do you think happened to me?" I ask.

Carlos slings his arm on the back of the bench and crosses his ankle over his knee. His lower legs are tan, poking out of his olive green shorts. He has a drawing of a key on his ankle. He rubs it absently with his thumb, but it doesn't wipe away. "I don't know. The infection in your port might have burned through the part of your brain that holds long-term memories. Or maybe you did have cancer, and the experimental high dose radiation they gave you cured you immediately but wiped all your memories. Or maybe you found out something you weren't supposed to, like you wandered into some secret nuclear test site or alien laboratory and the Feds erased your memory. If you wanna go the 'conspiracy theory' route, I can come up with dozens of 'em. But if we're keeping it simple, maybe the radiation and your memory issues have nothing to do with each other. Could be you just hit your head really hard when you crashed into my tent, and if I'd met you ten seconds before, you could have told me everything about yourself."

I stare at a gray brick building across the street. A woman saunters out, swinging a silver plastic bag from her wrist, and something about the motion makes my pulse throb faster for a beat. I shake my head and sigh. "Sometimes I feel like I'm about to have a flood of memories, like there's just a thin plastic film holding everything back, like it's all right there, just barely out of reach. It feels so familiar, like I've done it all before, like it's already happened once."

"Déjà vu?"

"Déjà huh?"

"What you're describing. That's what it's called. The feeling that something has happened exactly the same way before, and that you're reliving it."

"I didn't know there was a word for all that. But I should have, huh?"

Carlos shrugs. "Typically, yeah."

I raise my knees, putting my feet on the bench and wrapping my arms around them. "I feel like nothing about me is typical."

"You are definitely not run-of-the-mill."

"I'm going to use context clues and guess that's another phrase that means 'typical'?"

"You got it."

"Why does it mean that?"

"Hmm. Run-of-the-mill. Um, actually, I have no idea why it means that. Sounds like someone who's in charge of a mill when you really think about it."

I offer him a lopsided smile. "I guess I don't feel so bad for not knowing it if you can't explain it any better than that."

Carlos grins and stands up. "Come on. Why don't we walk around, and I'll show you all sorts of stuff you should already know. I'll do such a good job, you'll feel like you were born in this city."

"Okay. First question." I point to the creatures with spindly feet. "What are those?"

Carlos does a mediocre job of keeping his eyes from bugging out of his head. "Those are pigeons."

"And a pigeon is a…"

Carlos raises an eyebrow. "A bird."

I laugh in surprise. "No it's not."

Carlos knits his brows together and looks at me sideways. "Yes it is."

I chuckle again and shake my head. "A bird is a helicopter."

"Ha ha," Carlos drawls.

The look on his face stops me short. He honestly thinks I'm kidding around. "I'm really not joking," I say. "'Bird' is just a slang term for 'helicopter.'"

"Are you serious?"

I nod.

"How can you use the words 'context clues' correctly in a sentence and then thirty seconds later think a bird's a helicopter?"

I lift one shoulder. "I don't know. I can do other stuff, you know. Walk, breathe, pick locks. Maybe it's muscle memory or something. Maybe where I come from, we don't have birds."

"Impossible. Everybody has birds."

"Have you been everywhere?"

Carlos rolls his eyes. "No, but I just know. Birds are universal. And every city has pigeons. Some people call them rats with wings, but I kind of like them. They're tough. And, bet you didn't know this, doves are just albino pigeons. Everybody loves doves."

"You're right, I didn't know that. So" – I tick two fingers – "pigeons and doves are birds. Helicopters are too, but we can agree to disagree about that. What else do you have?"

"Want to go to the waterfront and meet some seagulls? Maybe a duck or two?"

"The water...front?" I ask, furrowing my brow.

"The beach? The shore? Where the land meets the sea? No?"

I shake my head to all of them.

"Maybe you're from Kansas?" Carlos claps his hands together and rubs them briskly. "Yes. You're from the dead center of the Midwest, where you lived a dry, bird-free existence, your boredom broken only by the drone of helicopters and the click of one successfully picked lock after another."

"Ha ha. You're hilarious. Is the waterfront...dangerous?"

"Not any more dangerous than any other part of the city. Probably less, because of all the tourists. It's just a little farther downhill."

I shudder involuntarily.

"Come on. It's fine," Carlos says, walking a few steps away and beckoning me to join him. "I'm not gonna let anything bad happen to you."

I glance behind me, up the hill, where somewhere cops are probably still looking for me, then back to Carlos's tall, rangy figure, grinning and crooking his finger at me. And somehow, I believe him. I place my palms on the bench and push myself to standing. "All right. Let's do it."

---

I stand on a weathered wooden dock and stare at a sparkling blue expanse in front of me. It shimmers and flashes in the sunshine, each little ripple in the water appearing to have a diamond on top. "You mean it just stays there? It doesn't come any closer?" I ask.

Carlos closes his fingers around the railing and leans his upper body over the moving water. I still haven't agreed to approach the edge, but the wood feels sturdy beneath my feet, and I shift a couple more inches toward him.

"Nope, tides don't seem to affect the shoreline here. I don't know why. I bet there's some scientific reason. It's deep through here. The ferries pull in over there" – Carlos waves his hand to the left – "and cruise ships too. Is that what scares you? The depth?"

"It's not the depth that scares me, I don't think. It's just water in general. I can't describe it. I feel like, I don't know, like it's toying with me."

Carlos gives me a questioning look.

"I can't explain it any better than that. It just doesn't feel right. It's dangerous and we shouldn't be so close to it. I have no idea what's lurking down there, but it's going to come roaring at us any second."

"Are you afraid of all water or just the ocean?"

"I didn't know there was more than one type."

"Sure. Oceans are salt water, lakes are fresh water."

"Fresh water is for drinking, so lakes should be fine. Salt water is the dangerous kind."

"Okay, so you're afraid of the ocean. That's different than being afraid of all water. The ocean goes all over the place in Seattle, but we can work around it. There're lots of places where you can't even see the ocean. We could head up to the U District, or Northgate. Those are both near Lake Washington, but that's fresh water, so it should be okay."

While Carlos has been talking, I've inched ever forward, and I've finally made it all the way to the rail. I grip it hard and force myself to look down. "No. I don't want to go anywhere. I don't want to be afraid of things. I have to face my fear, let it wash over me, and when it's gone, I will prevail."

"That's a good attitude." Carlos flexes his fingers and looks out over the water, and I force myself to do the same.

"Hey, Carlos?"

"Yeah?"

"Why are you being so nice to me? Wouldn't it be easier to just walk away?"

Carlos turns around, his back to the water, and puts his elbows on the railing. He looks up at the sky.

"You're an interesting conversationalist."

"No, I'm not. I'm a burden. I don't have any memories, I wrecked your tent, I was really sick, and the cops are after me."

"You have no safety net. That resonates with me. Plus, you remind me of someone who was important to me."

The weight of how alone I am hadn't hit me until now. His words surround me like the flock of pigeons in Pioneer Square, pecking at invisible chinks in my soul. I sniff back a lump in my throat. "You're right. I have no people. Other than the cops, no one came looking for me at the hospital, did they?"

Carlos shakes his head. "I'm sorry. I wish I could tell you different. They ran your stats and dental records against a bunch of databases, but no matches. It doesn't seem like anybody knows you're missing. Or if they do, they're not trying very hard to find you."

# CHAPTER ELEVEN

April 13, 2074

Davad Columbia stands on the 40th floor of his tower, stroking his chin pensively. It's been more than three weeks. Where is Rosie? What could have caused such a delay? He ticks through the points of her mission in his mind: tetanus boosters, sanitary napkins – a couple tasks, nothing too difficult. He stares at the wall in front of him, boring a hole in it with his eyes. The same beige wall as always, next to the mural of pre-Collapse Seattle. He flung out that last request to Rosie practically as an afterthought before he'd raced off to answer the Achtung. He sent his daughter on a time travel mission with a goodbye thrown over his shoulder. Now he can't even remember what the Achtung was about, and his daughter is missing.

*"Paint the wall blue,"* he told her. Repainting an interior wall was a luxury their limited resources couldn't afford, but every tower needed a blue wall, to give the citizens hope. It seemed like a brilliant move to have Rosie paint it in 2007. And if she'd done it, he'd be looking at a blue wall right now. To everyone else, it would have been their normal – what they grew up with. But not

to David. Since he was the one who gave Rosie the instructions to make the change and sent her on her mission, he would remember dual timelines. His mind would store memories of both the old, beige wall, and the new blue wall.

David grits his teeth. He doesn't want to send his daughter on these missions. But who can he trust? Anyone else he sent through time might simply choose to stay in the past and take their chances on surviving the Collapse. The further back they had to travel into the past to get the items they needed, the more of a lure it would be. The Collapse didn't occur until April 19, 2019. A traveler who went back to 1994 could get twenty-five good years. They could build a life. They could have children. *And who knows?* Armed with knowledge of the coming calamity, perhaps they could find a way to ride it out. Maybe there could be survivors beyond The Towers, if David would allow it. Should he? Send chrononauts back with the express purpose of never returning? Their mission to colonize other, better areas for long-term survival?

David runs his fingers through his dark hair. No. It's too much to think about. It's a miracle anyone lived beyond the first year of hell on Earth. His mother saved humanity, and it's his job now to make sure these few thousand humans in The Towers hang on, until the Earth recovers enough to walk it once more. There is no going back. There are no do-overs.

David glares at the wall and wills it to turn blue in front of him. It isn't about interior design or giving his citizens hope. It's about knowing Rosie is safe. A blue wall means she's out there, in 2007, taking care of business. It means she'll be home soon. "Where are you, Rosie?" David murmurs. "I need to know you're okay."

"David." Sarah's voice behind him startles him, but he controls his bodily response. His wife is one of the few people who can successfully sneak up on him. He supposes it's part of her attraction. She's different. Smooth. Sinuous. That's what he wants. Isn't it? That's part of what makes her interesting. But lately...David can't remember feeling anything for the woman. Why did he marry her?

David shakes his head, irritated. He is a man of action and assurance. Hesitation and second-guesses get you killed. This worry over Rosie is eating him alive. He composes his face, willing himself to erase the knots of concern from his countenance before he turns to his wife.

"You move like a panther."

"I know you love me, so I assume that's a compliment," Sarah purrs, one leg bent, her high-heeled shoe pressed against the wall behind her, a hand on one hip.

David's mouth twists into an approximation of a smile. "A panther was a big cat. It prowled jungles and rainforests a hundred years ago."

Sarah pushes her lip out in a pretty pout. "A big *animal*? Me?"

"It was just a term that meant they were predators. Panthers were silent and sleek." He closes the distance between them, puts his hands on her waist, and kisses her.

"That's better," Sarah breathes. "I've missed you, David. Are you starting to come back to me?"

"I haven't been anywhere."

"You know what I mean," Sarah says quietly, twining her hands around the back of his neck and kissing him again gently. "Since Rosie disappeared."

David's back stiffens, and he's silent for several long moments, but when he speaks, his voice is normal. "No one else has mentioned Rosie's absence," he replies calmly.

"Well, honey, nobody wants to upset you. No one's asked me about her, either. I'm sure they're waiting for a signal. Some sign that you're ready to talk about it, or even to move on. And..." She blushes prettily. "I have a suggestion about that."

David reaches back and gently removes her hands from

behind his head. He encircles her wrist with a loving hand and strokes her palm with one finger. "Do you?"

She draws a triangle shape on his chest with the index finger of her left hand. "I just had my fourth period...in a *row*," she says. "I know you loved Rosie, but I think you have to accept the fact that she's gone. It's a tragedy, honey, but she would want you to keep living. I'm ready, David. I'm healthy. I can have a baby. Your baby."

David smiles down into her face, his pleasant expression masking his racing thoughts. Sarah is inordinately tall for a citizen of The Towers, but he still has six inches on her. His mother sacrificed so much to make sure he received the proper nutrition to grow into a well-formed, powerful man, capable of leading humanity in its fragile, desperate state during its darkest hour of need. He named his daughter after her, and until Rosie came along, he never thought he could love someone as deeply as he loved his mother.

He cups Sarah's face in his hands, willing himself to touch her gently, when all he wants to do is seize her by the jaw and force her to spill everything she knows. "Let's go upstairs and talk about it."

# CHAPTER TWELVE

July 1, 2018

Carlos and I walk along the waterfront and I slowly begin to relax. I'm still afraid that a rogue wave will come out of nowhere and wash us away, but Carlos swears it won't happen, and none of the other hundreds of people walking around smiling and swinging their arms loosely seem to be worried at all. By the time we reach Wall Street and Carlos says we should turn right and head away from the water, I think there's been a miniscule reduction in my anxiety. I'm thrilled to be heading uphill, though, and I don't try to hide my relief.

A couple walk past us, the man pausing briefly at an open rectangle about waist-high. He deposits a Styrofoam container into the box. As soon as he walks away, Carlos snakes his hand in and plucks it deftly out.

"What a remarkable society," I marvel.

"How so?" Carlos asks dryly. He flicks the box open with his thumb, revealing light yellowish-brown sticks that smell heavenly.

"These boxes you have everywhere. Where people leave things if they don't need them so you can take them if you do. It's brilliant."

"Um, yeah. Sure."

"I call them 'leave one, take one' boxes in my head. What's the real word for them?"

"Trashcans."

"Huh. I had a trashcan in my room at the hospital, but they never put anything useful in it. They always brought me my food on a tray."

"Well, it's a multipurpose word, I guess."

"Another word that's been bumping around in my head is 'library.' What does that mean?"

"That's sort of like a 'leave one, take one' thing, except for it's not a can, it's a big building, and it's just for books."

I feel my eyes grow big. "Oh, I love books. I have three. I've read them each about a billion times."

Carlos and I both come to an abrupt halt. "Did you hear that?" I whisper. "I have three books."

"Which ones?"

"*Men to Match My Mountains* by Irving Stone, *The 100 Greatest Mysteries of All Time* by David Wallace, and *Sweet Valley High #4 Power Play* by Francine Pascal."

"Eclectic mix."

"Yeah. Books are hard to get where I come from. We don't have many. I don't know why I know that, but I'm sure of it. I love to read, though."

Carlos extends the Styrofoam box to me. "Want some fries?"

I dig a handful out and say 'yeah' at the same time. I stuff them in my mouth and they taste even more amazing than they smell. "Can you imagine," I say, "a whole room full of books?"

"There's a library up on Third. If you want, I'll take you there next. We can go in for a while, and when they close, we can spend the night nearby."

"I'd love that."

# CHAPTER THIRTEEN

April 13, 2074

Sarah tips her cup back and drains it. She shudders and licks her lips. "More."

David pours a glug into Sarah's cup, and she drinks it with identical greed. Her eyes shift out of focus for a moment, then stabilize. "I love alcohol."

"Have another."

Sarah drains her cup again, then staggers over to their queen-sized bed and sits down heavily. She kicks her high heels off and rotates her ankles, making twin cracking sounds. "I didn't know how long to wait to talk about having a baby. I thought it might be too soon after losing Rosie to bring it up. I'm glad I trusted my instincts." Her voice slows down. "I got good instincts."

"When did you first notice Rosie was gone?" David asks, sitting beside her and tucking a strand of her blonde hair behind her ear.

"Well, immediately, darling. You probably weren't aware how close Rosie and I had become in just the last few weeks before her disappearance."

"You're right, I wasn't."

Sarah fluffs her hair and crosses her legs at the knee. "We'd really begun to bond over girl stuff. She knew about my periods and she was thrilled. She was so excited at the idea of having a little brother. She really wanted a brother."

"You don't say."

"I'm sure she would have been happy for us either way, but I got the feeling she was worried another little girl might take her place in your heart. But we both know no one will ever replace Rosie." Sarah sniffs back a tear. "God, I miss her so much."

"You say you noticed she was gone immediately. Can you pinpoint the date?"

Sarah cocks her head up and to the right, thinking. "I don't remember what the date was. But I know it was the same day you received your last Achtung. She didn't come home that night. She hasn't been home since."

David drums his fingers on his knees. "Do you recall what that Achtung was about? Did I discuss it with you?"

"Of course not, honey, you never do. What a question!"

David stares at the wall opposite them. "I can't remember the contents of that Achtung myself. Doesn't that seem odd to you?"

"I'm sure the stress of losing Rosie has caused a lot of things to slip your mind. I was starting to worry that you'd forgotten that you love me too." Her tone grows sultry. "Let me help you remember."

Sarah stretches back on the bed. David lifts her left arm over her head, and she writhes with anticipation. He lies next to her and reaches into his back pocket, pulling out a thin strip of plastic. He slips the zip tie around her wrist with a rough yank and secures her to the bedpost.

"David," Sarah breathes, her voice catching with excitement, "you're full of surprises. I like it."

"Well, good." David grabs her other wrist and zip-ties it to the post too. "You may have to stay this way for a while."

Sarah's eyes widen, and she tries to sit up, but her hands are bound too tightly to the iron bedpost behind her.

David stands up. "Nobody has mentioned Rosie's absence," he says evenly, "because no one is aware of it. It's one of the rules. Only people directly involved in her disappearance have any idea she's missing. So how do you know she's gone, Sarah?"

# CHAPTER FOURTEEN

April 13, 2074

The helicopter's blades beat the air as the runners kiss the roof of Safeco Tower. Two men with rifles jump out and scout the area. Deeming it safe, one soldier turns and nods back at the helicopter. A figure emerges draped in opaque plastic sheeting. The soldiers advance, leading the way. By the time the figure moves across the roof and reaches shelter, the sheeting is beaded with fine droplets of moisture.

General Safeco opens the door to the roof's stairwell. The soldiers ID him by sight, and they snap salutes. The figure in plastic disappears into the stairwell, and the soldiers return to the helicopter. The blades slow to a stop, and they spend precious minutes draping the chopper with sheeting similar to that which had shrouded their passenger. They'll wait inside the helicopter until this meeting is over. Hopefully, it won't take long.

Safeco leads the arrival to a corner of the stairwell and helps David lift the plastic gently over his head, carefully folding it back and over itself, keeping the droplets of moisture away from David's skin. Neither man inhales nor exhales until the sheeting has been stuffed into a spinner. When the lid slams shut and Safeco presses the button to activate the decontamination cycle, David exhales the rest of his stored breath and takes a gulp of air.

"How long had you been holding your breath?" Safeco asks.

David bends at the waist and places his hands on his knees. "Twelve minutes."

Safeco cracks a rare smile. "You're getting old."

"You're one to talk," David says to his ancient friend.

"I'm not the one gasping like a fish out of water."

David laughs. "I'm not the one who remembers fish."

The two men shake hands and walk downstairs to Safeco's office, their feet squeaking on the linoleum floor. Light filters through the Gila screens, casting a grayish-green shadow, but Safeco ignores the floor lamp just inside the door.

David settles into one of two wing chairs next to a small round table. Safeco sinks into the other. "I was surprised by your visit," Safeco says. "I would have diverted power from the main electrical generator to my quarters if I'd had more time to prepare." He gestures to the floor lamp. "I've been running a skeleton system, just enough to run the coms and decon units on all floors. Main power's being funneled to hydroponics until the cabbage is ready to harvest."

David waves his hand in the air. "Don't ever risk a crop on my account."

Safeco seems pleased with the answer. "We tried growing several tomato plants with heirloom seeds. None bore fruit, but one did flower. Very promising."

"What were your takeaways from the experiment?"

Safeco taps his fingers on the arm of his chair. "Tomatoes prefer soil."

David nods absentmindedly and lapses into a long silence, which Safeco finally breaks. "I don't think you came here to talk about crops, and this isn't a social visit."

"Is it ever?"

A wry smile twists Safeco's lined face. "I thought on a Burn Level 2 day that you might bring your new wife over to meet me in person."

David's face settles into a hard mask. "She's currently bedridden."

"I'm sorry to hear that."

David shrugs. "Actually, she's part of the reason I'm here. This visit concerns my family."

Safeco drums his fingers on the arm of the chair. "The elephant in the room has made his appearance, and it didn't take long."

David bristles. "I tried, Enrique. But I couldn't run The Towers effectively and also disappear into the past for days at a time securing the things we need. You were lost. I hadn't seen you in years. I resigned myself to the belief that you'd never return. So I recruited my daughter, the one other person in this godforsaken world that I trust implicitly, to do those things in the past that I could no longer take care of myself."

"When I shared the formula with you, you swore a blood oath that you would never reveal it to another person."

"And I haven't. Rosie doesn't know the chemical formula or how to prepare it."

Safeco's eyes grow large and seem to protrude even further from his face. "And yet you send her into the past?"

"She goes with a pre-calibrated return dose that I prepare myself."

"What if she loses it, David?"

David stands up, his voice rising sharply, and directs his words at the seated General Safeco. "Don't you think I lie awake at night worrying about that?" He throws his hands in the air. "What was I supposed to do, Enrique? Let all of humanity die out because I can't risk the one person I love? What kind of a leader would I be then?"

Safeco stares at him, his eyes steady, his craggy face tightly controlled.

David rakes his hands through his hair, sits back down, and smooths his pant legs.

Safeco speaks quietly. "Faced with the same options, I may have done something similar. We've all sacrificed for this world."

David nods briskly. "Enrique, she's good at it. Rosie's already brought back enough multivitamins to cover our entire population for three years. Her only loss was a bag of water purification tablets."

"How many trips has she made?"

"She's on her seventh."

"Impressive." Safeco strokes the white stubble on his chin. "And she's traveling now?"

"Yes."

"I didn't miss her. Not that I would. I don't live in your tower."

"The same rules that we discovered hold true for Rosie when she's traveling. Nobody misses her. Events continue to occur and everyday life goes on, but Rosie's not mentioned...as if she has ceased to exist for everyone but myself and the prep team. But in this instance, there's one other person who remembers Rosie. My wife, Sarah."

Safeco's eyebrows zoom to the top of his forehead. "You let Sarah in on our secret? Isn't that rash? You barely know her."

David purses his lips and blows out a breath of air. "That's the thing. No, I haven't told Sarah anything about time travel, or the chronography program. Sarah isn't someone I would ever trust with a secret like that. I wouldn't trust her to tie my shoes. To be honest, I have no idea what attracted me to the woman, or why I married her in the first place."

Enrique wrinkles his brow. "Tell me what happened."

"Rosie left on March 21st in the early afternoon. She's been gone three weeks. This is the longest she's ever been gone on a mission. I have no evidence that she's making any headway. I've received no Achtungs. Nothing. Then, this morning, Sarah approaches me and long story short, she says it's time I admit that Rosie's lost and that I need to move on and start 'living my life' again."

"And you're sure she knows nothing of time travel? She couldn't be involved in any way with Rosie's current trip?"

"No, there's no possibility. I received an Achtung just as we finalized the details for Rosie's trip. She left for the prep room and I took a copter to Smith Tower to open the lockbox and retrieve the Achtung."

"Hmm. Perhaps what we thought were immutable rules of time travel are really more like guidelines."

"Do you really believe that?"

Safeco shakes his head. "No." He takes a deep breath. "But I don't have another explanation for it right now. I'll think on it. There must be something slightly different about this trip. When it comes to me, which I'm sure it will, I'll comm you on the secure line."

"And in the meantime, my daughter's missing, and the only people who know about it are myself and the prep team, now you, and for some unknown reason, Sarah. And I have to live with the fact that she may be dead or lost forever in 2007."

Enrique raises his eyebrows, a faint smile lighting up his face. "2007, you say?"

"Yes."

"And this is her seventh trip?"

David nods.

"What other time periods have you sent her to on her previous six trips?"

David answers readily. "1994, 1999, 2001 twice, 2003, and 2006."

"Then I believe I have some good news for you." Safeco stands and crosses the office to his desk. He slides open a drawer and pulls out a small stack of flat, quarter-inch thick sheaves of bound papers with glossy covers, only slightly faded by time. "I've wondered about this since I discovered it." He walks back to where David sits and places the objects on the small round table between them.

The words *"Sports Illustrated Kids"* are emblazoned across the top. Underneath is a focused young man in a blue jersey holding a football. A headline reads, "2007 NFL Preview." The date in the lower right corner is September 2007.

David's mouth drops open. "Magazines? Someone could purchase a small tower with these, they're worth a fortune, so few of them survived. Where did you find these? And in such good condition?"

"I noticed a spot in the corner of my office, over there." Safeco points to his left, where a corner of the wall is covered in strips of duct tape. "Just this morning, I walked into my office, and that area caught my eye. I thought to myself, *that wall looks patched*, when it never had before. So I took the claw end of a hammer and I checked it out. I pulled these out of the wall. And here's the most interesting part." Safeco rifles to about midway through the magazine, then spreads it open on the table and points to the top of the page. In the white top margin, written in blue ink, is a message. "Please give these to David."

David gasps.

"Is that Rosie's handwriting?" Safeco asks.

"It might be. Can I take this with me and compare it to a sample at home?"

"Of course."

David smiles, and lines seem to melt away from his face. "This is really encouraging. But why would she leave these in your office? And I sent her to April of 2007. How did she get ahold of a magazine from September of that year? Does that mean her mission is going to take more than four months? It must." David leafs through the other magazines. "And this one, *Ranger Rick*. It's from 2004. What does that mean? Is there a pattern? And how does Sarah factor into any of this?"

"She may, in fact, be trying to send you a coded message. As I recall, sometimes issues of magazines would come out one month ahead of time. So she may not be in September 2007. But she might. This is the order the magazines were stacked in. I haven't shuffled them. Take them back to your tower, analyze them. Perhaps she's communicating both time and location. You know her best. See what you can make of it."

David nods slowly. "I still don't understand why she'd hide them in your tower if they're for me."

Safeco holds his hands palms up. "Columbia Tower was always far more secure, back then, than Safeco. Perhaps she couldn't get to a place inside Columbia that she knew you'd discover. She's obviously a smart girl to come up with the idea to use this office to send a message if Columbia wasn't an option."

"Why is it so vague, though? Why didn't she send an Achtung?"

Safeco shrugs. "We don't know what she's experiencing in 2007, or what difficulties she may have run up against. But it's a good sign. As far as the April versus September issue, it could be a coded message. It could also mean she's in September of that year. Have you ever miscalculated a dose?"

David shakes his head. "Never."

Safeco furrows his eyebrows together. "There's a first time for everything, and perhaps this is it. Maybe you were a drop or two off on the dosage and she didn't travel as far back into the past as you expected. Have you spoken with the prep team?"

"No. For security reasons that you well know, I have as little contact with them as possible."

Safeco nods. "Once you're back in Columbia Tower, get them on the comm. Double check the dosage she received, and re-run your math. That may very well solve the mystery." He laces his fingers together and holds his hands lightly in his lap. "I know this is rough, David, but it's very encouraging. It tells you she's alive and that she has her mental faculties intact." He taps the side of his head. "I know all about that aspect of time travel."

David takes a deep breath and stands up. Safeco rises to join him. They clasp hands. "Thank you, Enrique. Thank you for your service, your unwavering commitment to the survival of The Towers, and on a personal level, for your friendship."

Safeco squeezes his hand hard. "You'll see your daughter again. I know it."

## CHAPTER FIFTEEN

July 1, 2018

The quiet is broken by a soothing robotic voice overhead. "The Seattle Public Library will be closing in fifteen minutes." I raise my head from my book and look around, blinking. Across from me, Carlos closes the book he's been reading. I do the same, sighing. "Can I take it with me?"

Carlos shakes his head. "No, I don't have a library card. You need one of those to check books out. But we can come back tomorrow and spend all day here if you want."

My eyes scan the shelves upon shelves of books. "There's not enough time in the world to read all of them. But I want to."

"How about we come back tomorrow, you finish that one, and then we'll see where we go from there?"

"Okay."

Carlos and I rise and wander through the rows of shelves, following the number system on the spines until we find the right locations for our books, which we slip back onto the shelf. "Did you like yours?" I ask.

"It was pretty good."

"What was it about?"

"A clown who lives in a sewer and the group of kids who fight him."

"What's a clown?"

Carlos grins. "Clowns are creatures made of pure evil."

I can't tell if he's joking with me or not. "My book was about a car that comes to life."

"Yeah, I've read that one. I liked it."

"I like it too. Can we really come back tomorrow so I can finish it?"

"Sure."

"I feel like I learned as much from that book as I did walking around the waterfront earlier."

"Maybe you don't need me after all? Gonna replace me with a bookbag?"

Now I'm sure he's joking with me. I elbow him in the side. "I'm not ready to do that just yet." We walk outside.

The colors are dazzling against the night sky. The traffic lights blaze against the city's dark backdrop, and glowing words shine out from nearly every shop window. "The art in the windows is so beautiful," I remark.

"Most people call them signs." Carlos points. "The 'open' and 'closed' ones are pretty common."

"Well they're wonderful. How do they get them to shine like that?"

"Neon gas."

"Never heard of it. Shocker."

Carlos smiles at me. "You're cute."

"That sounds like a compliment. Thank you."

He looks over his shoulder and digs his toe into the sidewalk. "It's getting late. We should find a little food and a safe place to spend the night."

"Do you want me to undo one of those locks, and we can just go inside?" I wave my hand at one of the shops with the 'closed' art in the window and a chain with a padlock securing two metal gates together that have been pulled across the business's main doors to block access.

"Nah, that's a gun shop. I think we're gonna want to stay away from that place."

"Guns! I know what those are." I step back a pace and eye the lock on the chain. "Are you sure you don't want me to get us in? That lock would be super easy."

"Yeah, hellraiser. I'm not looking for trouble and neither should you."

I shrug. "Okay. Maybe we should go back to your tent? Or is it too close to the hospital?"

A pained expression crosses Carlos's face. "My tent is gone."

I feel my eyes go round. "Oh no...I forgot about that. That's what you and Dez were arguing about at the hospital, right before everything went crazy. The cops tore down your tent while you were waiting for me to wake up. I'm so sorry. You lost everything because of me."

"It's okay. I'll rebuild." Carlos takes my hand, squeezes it, and doesn't let it go. "I'm a believer in 'everything happens for a reason.' If I'd been there at the tent, I'd probably have been dismantled along with it. They might've even arrested me on some trumped-up charge. I'm exactly where I'm supposed to be because I'm always where I'm supposed to be at every moment in time."

"That's really freaking optimistic."

Carlos smiles. "I have to be an optimist."

"Why?"

Carlos shrugs. "What's the alternative?"

"I suppose you could be consumed by bitterness and despair."

"I could. I've got enough reason to, that's for sure. But I decide how I react to things, and my choice is to laugh in life's face and tell it if it wants to crush me, it's gonna have to try harder than that."

"That sounds like a dangerous challenge."

Carlos cocks his head. "Nah. I don't believe in fate or anything. I don't think there's some unavoidable destiny that I can't do anything about. I'm just saying I roll with the punches."

I nod, but a thread of uneasiness twists through my body. I *do* believe in fate. I *do* believe in destiny. And I don't know why, but I am absolutely not an optimist.

# CHAPTER SIXTEEN

April 13, 2074

Davic packs his lungs with air and dons his protective sheeting to prepare for the trip back to Columbia Tower. As soon as he thrusts the roof door open, the two soldiers emerge from his helicopter, push their way through the sheeting that protects the helicopter, and yank it down. They fold it expertly and stow it in the tail of the craft. They stand sentinel on either side of the door while David climbs in, then they follow him inside. David remains under the sheeting for the ride to Columbia, which takes just a few minutes.

They're hovering and just beginning their descent when David hears the crackle of the comm. It's nearly drowned out by the whump of the rotors and further muffled by his protective sheeting.

"Be advised, Chopper B, food riot in progress, level thirty-five. Stairwells compromised on thirty-four, thirty-five, thirty-six, and thirty-seven."

The heaviest soldier immediately addresses the pilot. "Abort landing."

David throws off his protective sheeting and exhales in a burst of words. "Put this bird down right now."

"Sir, there's a food riot in progress. Four compromised stairwells."

"I heard. I am the leader of this Tower and I will not hide in the airspace above it. I'm going in."

The pilot nods and speaks into her comm. "I have David Columbia aboard. We are putting down and joining the quell."

"Roger that, Chopper B."

The helicopter makes a hurried descent and bumps hard against the helipad. David doesn't waste time packing his lungs with air and covering his body with the plastic sheeting. He grabs a rifle and slings it over his shoulder so that it rests across his back. "We'll rappel in through the straws." He points at one soldier. "Roman, you're shaft A." He points to the other soldier. "Victor, you're shaft B. I'll take shaft C."

The pilot takes off her helmet and grabs a fourth gun from the rack. "I'll go first down C. Follow me in thirty seconds."

David holds his hand out in front of himself to stop her. "No. You're the best pilot I've got. I'm not going to risk losing you."

"But, sir, we can't risk you, either."

"I wasn't always the leader of this tower. Before we lost my mother, I was a soldier. You're to shield this copter and then shelter in place in the safe room on the seventy-second floor until you receive further instructions. That is an order."

The pilot dips her head. "Yes, sir."

David turns to Roman and big Victor. "Remember, do not use lethal force unless it's absolutely necessary. Shoot to stun only."

Roman and Victor exchange puzzled glances. Roman speaks for both of them. "I'm sorry, sir, but *what?*"

"I said non-lethal force only. If you must shoot, aim for the extremities. Stop and drop, but do not kill."

"Sir, with all due respect, these are insurgents. You've always said we're not going to waste any resources patching up wounded terrorists."

David glares at Roman, irritated. "I would never say that. You heard my orders. You know the plan. We go on my mark. Three, two, one, now!"

The men drop out the helicopter's side door and sprint for their respective shafts. David dashes from shaft to shaft, pressing his thumb for several seconds against different lockpads, which cause them to spring open and reveal giant coils of sturdy nylon rope. At shaft C, he jumps lightly into a body harness and fastens it around his hips. He pops open another lockpad with his thumb and grabs the lightweight nylon cord coiled at his feet, then hurls it down the elevator shaft. It falls for a few seconds, then hangs taut against the heavy metal rings that secure it to the roof's surface. David clips a specialized carabiner from his harness to the cord, climbs to the top of the elevator shaft, and then jumps straight down the center. Air rushes past him as he freefalls for several moments. He yanks on the carabiner and his descent slows. Glowing numbers on the nylon cord come into focus. Sixty-seven, sixty-six, sixty-five. David increases his speed again for a moment. Forty-one, forty, thirty-nine. David lowers himself until he reaches the glowing number thirty-five. He cinches the carabiner and comes to a stop.

Thirty-five is a closed-door floor, as nearly all of them are, but David has done this maneuver a thousand times. He swings his arms and legs in opposite directions until he's swaying from side to side. Three more pendulum swings back and forth, and his feet touch one of the walls. Straightening his knees he shoves himself away from the wall and over to the opposite side, where he lands and perches on the inches-wide interior ledge of the elevator doors. He slips his fingers in the crack between the metal doors, forces them open, and swiftly leaps through, lithe and catlike, despite his age.

"Intruder!" David's head snaps to the left and he absorbs a punch from his blind side. He flips his rifle from his back into his hands, twirls it around, and rams the butt end into the face of a man trying to wrap his hands around David's waist in a tackle. The man falls like a ragdoll, several of his teeth littering the carpet when his head makes rough contact with the ground.

Save for the now-unconscious man, the hallway is deserted. David advances to the right, his gun held ready in front of him. He knows this building inside and out. It's been his home for his whole life. He kicks the door of the storeroom on his left open, rifle at the ready.

"Don't shoot. We're not a part of this," a man cries.

David nods briskly. "Stay quiet, shelter in place. I'm locking you in for your own safety." David closes the door, reaches into his pocket, and pulls out a strip of plastape, which he affixes across the doorjamb. It hardens instantly.

He moves to the next room, which stands empty. One more empty room, and he's cleared the hallway. Shaft C didn't lead him into the heart of the action, but shouts and sounds of a scuffle reach him from the other side of the building, where Roman, coming from Shaft A, should be now. David hurries across the building. He passes a couple of terrified women who flatten themselves against the wall as he rushes by, and he pays them no mind. The noises he's been following have died down to nothing.

*Click-thunk.* The unmistakable sound of a rifle being cocked makes him pick up his pace. He turns the corner and stops abruptly, his jaw dropping open for half a second before he snaps it shut.

Victor and three other guards with guns are holding a group of six men and women, bunched in a tight knot of humanity, at gunpoint. A seventh man is on his knees at Roman's feet. Roman's rifle is an inch from his temple. The man's eyes are squeezed shut, his teeth clenched, with beads of sweat pouring down his face.

Roman doesn't take his eyes off the man when he speaks to David. "Sir, the stairwells are secure and it was a relatively small insurrection. If you'd rather not waste ammunition, we can transport these insurgents to the roof and throw them off."

David unclenches his jaw. "Roman, stand down."

Roman still doesn't move his eyes from his prisoner. "Excuse me, sir?"

"I said *stand down.*"

"We have to deal with these terrorists, Mr. President."

"This man is skin and bone. These are hungry people. When is the last time any of you were fed?"

A woman in the small group of people speaks courageously, her voice squeaking from the effort. "Nine days. No one on thirty-five has received a food allotment for nine days."

Victor responds immediately. "Sir, she's lying. Everyone in Columbia receives their food allotment every three days, per regulations."

"We haven't," a captive man retorts. "And we've pursued all the official channels with no results. We're starving to death down here."

"Guards." David Columbia's voice is firm. "You will escort the prisoners to the west-facing conference room outside of Shaft A, where they will be held, unharmed, until I complete an investigation into this matter. In the meantime, I want you, and you" – David gestures to two of the other guards – "to get these people some fracking food. There are a number of others sheltering in place on this floor. Make sure they're fed as well."

The man with the gun to his head bursts into tears. "Thank you, sir," he sobs over and over.

Roman lifts his gun, pointing it at the ceiling. "You can't trust these people, sir. They're rebels. They *blocked a stairwell.*"

"You held a gun to a man's head for blocking a stairwell? My god."

"No blocking of stairwells, sir. It's the rule. It's been a capital offense for more than fifty years."

David holds his head and takes a deep breath. "I'm aware of the rule, but in this case I'm making an exception. This isn't a riot. It's a demonstration."

"Sir, with all due respect, a riot and a demonstration are the same thing. You know that."

David shakes his head. "The prisoners will be escorted to the west-facing conference room outside Shaft A and fed – now. That's an order."

Roman knits his eyebrows together. "Yes, sir."

David climbs the south stairwell, sorting through his list of follow-up tasks to the rhythm of his steady footfalls. His first stop will be floor seventy-two to release his pilot from the safe room. He'll task her with retracting the nylon cords from the shafts; right now they're an open invitation. But when he reaches the landing on the fortieth floor, he pauses. Instead of continuing up, he pushes the heavy fire door open to the main floor and makes his way to the mural of old Seattle.

He stands in front of it and reaches inside the flap of his jacket to pat the magazines that have been tucked into his inside pocket since he left Safeco Tower. He still doesn't know what caused Rosie's delay, but at least he knows she's safe. He stares at the mural for another minute. He has important, time-sensitive work to do, and he knows he has to get on it, but he can't seem to drag himself away. He's stood before this mural a thousand times. He knows every loop, every contour, every tiny pixelated dot in the entire installation. And something is wrong. He can't put his finger on it, but something is off. Something is different about the mural this time. He steps back several paces until his shoulder blades are pressed against the opposite wall to get the best view possible. He lets his eyes go slightly unfocused. The images jumble and waver in front of him, and the discrepancy pops out. David advances to the mural, drops to his knees, and with a trembling finger, he traces the words scrawled in black ink in the lower right corner of the mural.

*Help me Daddy.*

# CHAPTER SEVENTEEN

## July 1, 2018

Four blocks later, Carlos is still holding my hand, and I'm letting him. The walk light is on, but it changes to a blinking red hand just as I step off the curb. A car rushes around the corner, heedless of my presence in the street. Carlos yanks me backward and swears softly. "We gotta hunker down for the night. I'm going to introduce you to some friends of mine; there's safety in numbers. You might remember one of my friends. You've met him before."

"Dez?"

Carlos shakes his head. "No. Dez is gone. But I'm glad you remember him. It shows that you don't have short-term memory issues, so that's great."

"Optimist."

"Always."

I feel a glow in the center of my body. I might not remember much of anything from before I met Carlos, but at least I'm making and storing new memories, and so far, a lot of them are pretty good.

I wrinkle my brow. "I was really out of it at first, so maybe I'm wrong, but I kind of remember Dez not liking me very much."

"To be fair, you did collapse a tent on top of him while he was sleeping."

My heart thuds, shoving pulses of blood so hard through my body that I can literally feel my veins expanding and contracting. "Collapse?"

Carlos laughs, not noticing my panic, or how gray my skin must have turned with all the blood rapidly pooling in my organs. "It's okay. He's had worse. We might see him again someday once he cools off. No, tonight we're going to stay where my friend Kevin does."

The sign switches from a glowing red hand to a white 'WALK' and I try to make my legs work to ferry me across the street with Carlos, but my knees won't bend. Carlos tugs at my inert body. "We got the walk."

I stare at him and will myself to go, but all I'm able to do is shake my head in a tiny movement from side to side.

He keeps hold of my hand but no longer tries to drag me across the street. "It's okay. Kevin's a good guy. You met him at Goodwill."

I blink my eyes rapidly. Slowly, my body is coming out of paralysis, and finally I'm able to choke out a few words. "It's not that."

Carlos strokes my hand gently. "Then what is it?"

I stutter. "I...I...I don't know. Something you said scared me."

Carlos wrinkles his brow, trying to remember his words. "About you falling on the tent?"

I grit my teeth and force a nod, but it's easier to move now. My fear is receding, the panic ebbing away from the surface of my skin, and I breathe and feel my extremities begin to come back to life. "Yeah, but it wasn't exactly that. Something about it, though. I can't put my finger on it."

"We still don't know how you ended up on my tent. Maybe

you're starting to remember a little bit about that night and how you got there?"

I search my brain, grasping for any threads of memory that would explain my out-of-nowhere panic attack, and I slowly shake my head. "No, I still have no idea. Something you said just froze me, and I don't know why. I'm sorry."

"You don't have to apologize, Boo. We don't know what you went through, but it had to be bad. Maybe we should find someplace to bed down for the night, just us."

"No, you said there's safety in numbers, and I believe you. I'm better now."

"You sure?"

I flex my fingers and shake my wrists. "Yeah." I cock my head at him. "Did you just call me 'Boo'?"

Carlos looks flustered. "Um, yeah. I guess I did." He rushes on defensively. "There was this movie I saw when I was a kid where this girl with brown hair accidentally winds up living in a monster world, but there's this good monster who takes her under his wing, and he calls her 'Boo.' I guess it's been bumping around in my head that you're kind of like that girl. Tiny, cute, and lost. It slipped out."

I squeeze Carlos's hand. "I like it a lot better than 'Lita.'"

---

At first, when Carlos brings me over to his campfire under the University Street overpass, Kevin doesn't believe I'm the same person he met at Goodwill. I guess my look has changed now that I'm not sick. The red dress fits me differently, that's for sure, and I remember Doctor Blank told me I grew significantly taller just in the one week that I was in the hospital.

People come and go, warming themselves by the flames of Kevin's fire, then drifting off. It takes Kevin nearly an hour to eat a sandwich. He tucks his food away protectively whenever anyone new approaches. While he has a joke and a smile for everyone, it's obvious that he has trust issues.

When the fire dies down to coals, Kevin nods at us. "G'night, you two."

I stare at Carlos. I haven't thought about the sleeping situation until now. Am I supposed to go find my own place to curl up, like some of the others beneath the overpass, tucked into niches in the concrete with newspapers pulled over their heads to keep them warm, or are Carlos and I supposed to keep each other warm? I feel a blush creeping into my cheeks. I don't know how things work in this city, but I instinctively know that sleeping next to Carlos would mean something more than just two people who haven't found enough newspaper.

Carlos clears his throat. "Um, I usually sleep over there," he says, pointing at a scraggly bush growing defiantly out of a large crack in the concrete. "There's room enough for two, but I can help you find your own spot if you want."

"I feel like I'd be safer with you."

Carlos nods. "You would."

"Let's do that then."

"No funny business," Carlos says solemnly. "I promise."

And he's true to his word. Carlos and I crawl under the bush, he lies down first, and I stretch out beside him. He rolls onto his side, wraps his arms around me, and I nestle my head on his bicep. I whisper a goodnight, and I count the whooshing sounds of cars rushing past us overhead. I don't even make it to ten before I'm fast asleep.

It's still full dark when I pop awake. Carlos told me that the sounds of cars would pick up as dawn approached to the point that I wouldn't be able to hear them individually – it would just be a loud thrum of constant noise. I know that it must not be close to dawn yet because I count a rushing sound about once every fifteen to twenty seconds.

Carlos shifts in his sleep and I twist around to peer intently into his face. In sleep, he looks younger, as if he doesn't have a care in the world. I stare at him for a few moments longer, wondering what his story is. I've been so focused on my memory issues, I realize I know very little about him.

He sighs in his sleep and a wrinkle appears between his eyes. I want to rub it until he's at peace again, but I don't want to wake him. Afraid I won't be able to resist the temptation to smooth the wrinkle, I slither out of his arms, which is pretty easy to do because I'm much smaller than he is and I'm still wearing the slippery red dress. I crawl out from under the bush and shiver with a sudden chill.

I realize I need to find another bush, one that I can use discreetly, so I tiptoe away from Carlos in search of a little more privacy.

There are people everywhere under the overpass, not all of whom are sleeping, and I give them a wide berth. I finally find a spot where I feel comfortable, away from people, and I take care of business.

I want to see the cars that make the thrumming noise above me, so when I'm done, I don't return immediately to Carlos's scrappy bush. Instead I strike out in a different direction until I'm clear of the overpass. I look up, and I sink to my knees. My mouth drops open and I wipe at my eyes. My fists come away damp. I'm utterly dazzled by the night sky. Stars. These must be stars.

"Boo?"

Carlos's voice snatches me back to where I am.

"Isn't it beautiful?" I breathe.

Carlos's voice is tight. "I watched you walk away. I thought you weren't coming back...and I was just going to let you go. But then I saw you stop, like you couldn't decide. And I came out to get you. I don't want to make that mistake again. I don't want you to leave."

I rip my eyes away from the night sky. "I'm not leaving,

Carlos. But have you seen this?" My voice thickens. "It's so amazing."

Carlos sinks down beside me and takes my hand. "What is it?"

"The stars."

"Oh, baby." Carlos sighs. "You can't see stars in the city."

I blink rapidly and shake my head. "You can't? What are those then?" I ask, waving my arm above me in a sweeping arc.

"Office windows."

"Wow," I breathe. "Windows don't look like that where I come from." An image of tall, dusky, grayish-green skyscrapers floods my mind and I close my eyes. I flex my fists involuntarily, as if I can grab the fleeting mental image, shake it, and make it tell me everything, but it's already receded back to the recesses of my mind.

"You make the world a magical place, Boo. I can't wait until you do see stars."

My eyes fly open and hope surges in my chest. "Can you? Are they real?"

Carlos nods, and his face seems to glow from within, though I know it's just the light from the office windows shining down on us.

"On a clear night, if you get far enough away from the city, you can see stars."

"How many?"

"Thousands. Millions."

"Will you take me to see them?"

Carlos cups my chin in his hands. "I promise."

I smile and look up at him through my lashes. "I believe you."

I step back and lace my hands together in front of my body. "What's your story, Carlos?

Carlos shifts his eyes away from mine, and his lips press together. "How did I become homeless, do you mean?"

"I want to know how you became you, so if that's where you want to start, then I want to hear it. I can't go back to sleep after that." I wave my arm in the air toward the office windows. "I'm up for the day."

"Hopefully, my tale of woe won't put you right back to sleep."

"You could never bore me."

"That might be the nicest compliment I've ever gotten." Carlos looks like he's going to smile for a second, but then he quirks his lips down. "Let's go get our stuff."

I follow him back to the scraggly bush. He crawls underneath and emerges with his backpack.

He and I scramble down the pockmarked concrete slope of the underpass until we reach the sidewalk. I match his step and we walk slowly along the quiet pre-dawn streets. I don't prompt him for his story again. I know he'll start talking when he's ready. It doesn't take long.

"My family was normal, before. Me, Mom and Dad, my little brother, Ricky. We had a house with a yard. We loved baseball and hated homework and Ricky wouldn't eat anything unless it was round." Carlos snorts. "Mozzarella balls, oranges, grapes, sandwiches cut into a circle. Everything had to be round." He kicks his toe on the sidewalk. "Then Mom got cancer. I was nine when she was diagnosed. Ricky was six. They tried everything, but the cancer was really aggressive. She was in and out of the hospital, and after two years, she died."

I blink slowly and my throat feels dry. "I'm so sorry."

"Me too," Carlos says softly. "She was a great mom." His voice strengthens. "Anyway, my parents spent all the money they had on medical bills. Mom was on a ton of medications, and chemo made her feel terrible. My dad decided to grow a little marijuana, just a few plants, for her to use. It helped her with pain and nausea." He pauses. "Dad lost his job while she was sick, he took too much time off taking care of her. After she died, Dad kept growing. He added more plants. He was good with them, and he knew a couple of guys who were willing to pay cash for whatever he harvested. It ended up becoming a full-time job, and it paid the rent. Until the day he got busted."

"Busted?" I ask. From the somber note in his voice, I had a pretty good idea what that meant.

Carlos's tone turns bitter. "Pot's legal now. But it wasn't when he was growing it. It became legal before Dad even went to trial. But he's brown and he had a public defender. He got twenty-five years in federal prison. I was twelve."

"Oh, Carlos. You've lived on your own since then? What happened to your little brother?"

Carlos shifts. "I didn't live on my own, at first. Me and Ricky got put into foster care."

"What's that?"

"It's when the cops send kids to go to live with strangers because their own parents can't do it."

"Sounds weird."

"Yeah, it kind of is."

"You said I reminded you of your foster sister," I say, recognition dawning in my voice.

"Yeah. Ricky and I got split up. One of Mom's favorite nurses was a licensed foster care provider, and she wanted us both, but the state wouldn't let her. They said her apartment wasn't big enough. Ricky went with her because he was younger, and I'm glad he did because I know he's safe."

"So Ricky's still there? With the nurse?"

Carlos nods. "Yeah. He's sixteen now and just finished his sophomore year of high school."

I'm not sure what that is, but Carlos's voice is full of pride, so I know it's a good thing. "Where did you go?" I ask.

Carlos shrugs. "I bounced around. Six different places the first year." He reaches into his pocket and pulls out a metal disk, which he flips into the air and catches. "I spent about a year in a group home when I was thirteen, but when I was fourteen I found my forever home." Carlos's voice has turned sarcastic and he rolls his eyes. "That was where I met Rachel."

Somewhere nearby, a pigeon coos. The neon around us is less vibrant in the filtered gray light of dawn. There are more people on the sidewalk now, their pace faster than ours.

"She's the one I remind you of?"

"Yeah. She was seventeen but really small for her age. I was fourteen and I thought I was older than her at first. She'd been there a few years and showed me the ropes."

"You'd already been in foster care for a couple years, though, right? So why did you need her help? What was different about that place?"

"My foster parents were an older couple. They had an adult daughter with cerebral palsy that they needed help taking care of. So instead of hiring a nurse, they got foster kids. Rachel was really good with her, but she couldn't lift her from her wheelchair or get her in and out of the bathtub. They picked me from a list because I was six feet tall and a hundred and eighty pounds. The medical knowledge I'd picked up from being in the hospital with Mom was an unexpected bonus for them."

Carlos reaches out and squeezes my shoulder. "Come on. Let's go find some breakfast before the sun is all the way up. Better cover if you need to pick a lock."

I scoff. "I don't need cover." I follow him down a narrow opening between tall buildings, and sure enough, there's a lock on the large trashcan box that Carlos calls a 'dumpster.' I pick it easily and he unthreads the chain. He lifts the lid and a cloud of insects swarm up, along with a horrid smell.

Carlos slams the lid back down. "Ugh, diapers. Bet this place has a basement daycare."

"I thought people only put stuff you could use in these things," I say, waving my hand in front of my nose to clear the air. "That smells like a six-and-under floor."

Carlos looks at me quizzically but tilts his head at the next dumpster over. "Pretty soon, I'm going to have to explain the concept of garbage to you, but I want to enjoy your innocence for just a little longer. Try this one."

I pick the lock on that dumpster and the contents are far more acceptable. Carlos and I pull out a bunch of brown curved things that he calls bananas and a good-smelling container of bread, which we split.

He pulls his backpack off, wraps up half his share of the bread and tucks it inside, along with two of the bananas. "For later," he says, hitching his backpack over his shoulder.

I can always pop a lock on a dumpster to get food later, but maybe he's expecting more trouble with diapers. Unconsciously, I move to tuck some of my bread into an inside pocket of my vest before I remember the vest is gone and I'm still wearing the slippery red dress. I look down at myself ruefully. "I think I need a change of clothes."

Carlos nods. "Later we'll go back to Goodwill. Kevin's working there today. We'll get you something more durable. Keep the dress, though."

I nod. I love this dress in a way that I can't explain. "I should have a backpack too," I say.

Carlos agrees. "They don't always have those, but we'll find you something – at least a satchel for now."

I pop the last of my bread in my mouth and lick my lips. "So tell me more about the foster place where you lived. What happened? Why are you here now and not still there?"

Carlos turns a corner onto Spring Street. "My foster parents weren't great people or anything. They weren't the biggest jerks I ever met in the system, but they aren't humanitarians. They get paid for every foster kid they take in. So I was working for them, taking care of their daughter for free, and they were getting a paycheck from the state to cover the cost of 'raising' me. I didn't go to school; they had a homeschool certificate so I didn't have to. I just worked all day long." Carlos shrugs one shoulder. "When

I turned eighteen, they kicked me out and moved in another teenage kid who was also tall for his age. I would have left anyway." He sticks his thumbs under his backpack straps. "So it's fine. I'd rather take my chances out here."

I wrinkle my brow. "What ever happened to Rachel?"

"They kicked her out three years before me. She gave me her email address and said to stay in touch. I don't know why she did that; she knew it wouldn't happen. We weren't allowed to use the computer at the foster home, like they were afraid we'd report them or something. As if anyone would listen to us."

"They have computers at the library. I saw them yesterday. You could email her now, couldn't you?"

"I suppose. She's twenty-two now. She probably doesn't remember me, and even if she did, she's got her own life to live. She doesn't need some homeless punk kid asking her for a couch to crash on."

"Yeah, but that isn't what you'd be doing. I think you should email her."

Carlos waves his hand at the sidewalk. "Her email might not even work anymore."

He seems to be growing more irritable and I feel like I should probably back off, but I can't stop myself from trying once more. "How will you know unless you try?"

"I don't know, okay? She could be dead for all I know."

And I realize the source of Carlos's fear. It's the not knowing. Right now, Rachel's simply lost, so she can be anything. She can be healthy, happy, and successful. He cares about her. He doesn't *want* to find out the truth. He prefers the dream, so I drop it.

I recognize our surroundings. "Are we going back to the library?" I ask hopefully.

"That's what I said we'd do, isn't it?" Carlos says, and I can tell he's still ruffled, but he softens his words with a grin. It fades, however, as we take a couple more steps down the hill. "Ah, crap."

"What?" I ask, scanning the street for the source of Carlos's dismay.

"Cops," he says.

"Where?" I bounce on tiptoes, as if I could see them if I were just a little taller.

"Over there," Carlos says, grabbing my elbow and steering me in a different direction, so that the rising sun is on our left now. "Don't draw their attention. I'm sure they're not there for us or anything, but you did *just* escape from the hospital yesterday. No need to tempt fate." Carlos purses his lips. "Damn. I have to go to the bathroom. We shouldn't go in there now, though, not with that many cops around. Not too many places downtown with a public bathroom, but I know a good one just a few blocks away. Close to where I first met you, actually. Come on. You'll like it. It's got a great view."

Twenty minutes later, Carlos and I stride through wide glass doors and into a high-ceilinged marble lobby. "There's three sets of elevators here. We have to get on the right one, the one that goes to forty. There's a coffee shop on that floor and a public restroom where no one ever hassles you as long as you don't act like a freak." He leads me to the center of the building and presses a button with his index finger.

My pulse pounds in my neck. It feels like my heart has crawled up to the top of my throat.

"I know you don't like elevators, but it's really fast and smooth and the view is seriously incredible."

A bell dings, the doors slide open, and I allow myself to be led inside. My legs refuse to bend at the knee, just like last night in the crosswalk, so I waddle. Carlos squeezes my hand. The other passengers pointedly ignore us. The elevator doors close and my stomach whooshes up and down inside my body as we're rocketed upward. I close my eyes.

They're still closed when the bell dings again and Carlos pulls me forward. My legs still aren't working right.

"Open your eyes," he whispers, not unkindly.

I do, and I gasp. Carlos has led me over to a window, and from here, I can see the whole city. It looks wrong. There shouldn't be so many buildings. But there are. Dozens of roofs are visible below us, and when I crane my neck and peer down, I see all the way to the streets, which are full of tiny cars, and even smaller, little moving specks that I know must be people.

"Where's all the water?" I ask in a tremulous voice.

"Over there," Carlos beams, pointing.

I follow his finger and see the sparkling strip of blue. "It's... beautiful," I whisper. I never expected that word to pop out of my mouth about water, but it hovers in the air between us until all the blood rushes to my head and I wobble on my feet.

"Whoa," Carlos says, steadying me. "Vertigo. You should sit down."

"Can I?" I ask.

"Yeah, if it's just for a minute, they won't hassle you. You can sit at any of those empty tables while you wait for me. I won't be long." He hurries down a hallway back in the direction of the elevators.

I trip-stumble to a small table with two empty chairs on either side. A man in a green apron works a loud machine. Somehow I know that he's making coffee. I've seen somebody do this before. I just can't remember when. The man sets a white cup on an oval counter. "Half-caf mochaccino for Corbley," he calls out.

"Courtney?" says a woman, her voice rising to make her word a question.

"Sure thing." The man laughs. "You know how we are."

His arms fly at the machine he works, whirring and grinding

noises emanating from various parts of the apparatus. He's making coffee. I saw someone else doing it yesterday. A balding man in a green apron appears behind him. "Ready for your break?" he asks.

"Is the Pope Catholic?" the first man responds. "I'm ready to collapse."

The floor tilts underneath me. I grip the table's edge hard and pull myself to standing. "What did you say?" My voice trembles.

The men stare at me, but neither one responds to my question. "Are you waiting for something, sweetie?" the balding man says. He gives me a sympathetic look. "Would you like a cup of ice water?"

I shake my head and stagger away from the men, around a slight angle in the wall. I stop short and stare. There in front of me is a huge full-wall photograph of the city. I know this picture. I reach out and brush it with my fingertips, my heart and my head pounding. I whirl around and go back to the coffee counter. "What year is it?" I blurt. I hadn't realized I was going to speak until the words are already out there.

The bald man is the only one working now. "2018," he says. "Let me get you that water."

He scribbles something on a paper cup with a black marker and sets it down, then turns away to get me a water. I grab the marker and dash back to the giant photo of the city. My knees decide that they're done holding me up, and I crash onto them at the base of the photo. I uncap the pen and scrawl the only thing I can think of. Then Carlos is there, hauling me to my feet and rushing me down the hallway and into a stairwell. I think I hear angry voices behind us.

Stairs. *No one can beat me on stairs.* I grab Carlos's hand. I refuse to leave him behind. I run as if Death himself is grasping at my shoulders, his breath heavy and hot on my neck.

# CHAPTER EIGHTEEN

April 13, 2074

*elp me Daddy.*

H The phrase ricochets in David Columbia's head like a ping pong ball shot out of a highspeed cannon. He told her to paint a wall blue. Instead, she'd defaced the mural next to it and sent a desperate cry for help across a sixty-seven-year gulf.

And she must have just done it, wherever she is now. He'd scrutinized the wall next to this mural yesterday, hoping for something, anything, to let him know Rosie was still alive. Now he almost wished he hadn't.

No. "Help me Daddy" wasn't good, obviously, but it meant that at least as of yesterday, she was still alive, and on the fortieth floor of Columbia tower, at least briefly. There was hope.

All thoughts of his pilot in the safe room and his post-food-riot duties have to go on the back burner. Rosie needs him. He still doesn't know how Sarah figures into all this. And why had Rosie planted magazines inside Safeco's office wall from

September of 2007? It's his best clue, so at least he knows where he needs to start.

David doesn't stop to comm ahead. He rushes down the south stairwell. He knows they'll be there, waiting for him, twenty-four hours a day, seven days a week. It's their job.

Beverly is on guard duty. She levels her weapon when he bursts out of the stairwell but lowers it quickly. "Sir," she barks, snapping a salute.

David flashes her a quick one in return. "Get me scanned in. I don't have a moment to waste."

Beverly runs his fingerprints quickly, and he jabs in his three-digit code. As soon as the door slams shut behind him, Lisa is at his side.

"Sir," Lisa says. "Welcome back. Are you traveling today?"

David shakes his head. "No. I've come to ask you some questions about Rosie's last trip."

"Of course," Lisa says. "Come into the control room and I'll pull the records. I can offer you any data you need."

"Thank you."

David and Lisa move to the control room behind the thick glass panel. The hairy-armed chemical man joins them. David nods at him. "Doug."

Doug nods back and taps his forehead in greeting.

Lisa reaches into a file cabinet drawer and pulls out a manila folder thick with precious paper. The sheets are filled with cramped, handwritten notes. "Okay," she says. "I've got the file."

David tilts his head, thinking back to the magazines pulled from Safeco's office wall. "I need you to start by double checking my calculations on the chemicals. Is there any possibility that Rosie may have stopped a little short of her distance? Say, landing in September 2007 rather than June?"

Lisa stares at the paperwork, her brow wrinkling as an odd expression crosses her face. "I'll double check the math, sir, but I'm not sure I completely understand your question."

"What do you mean?"

Lisa speaks slowly. "Well, sir, landing in September of 2007 would be more than a year short of her goal, not just 'slightly.'"

A strange feeling worms its way through David's intestines, like he's swallowed a live animal. "A landing in September 2007 would put her just three months off her destination."

"But, sir," she pushes back, "her last trip was to April of 2006." She flips her paperwork to the next-to-last page of the file, scans it, and looked earnestly into David's eyes. "She traveled to the fifteenth and returned four days later, landing in Safeco Tower due to extenuating circumstances with law enforcement in '06. If you're concerned she fell short of her destination and arrived in September rather than April, you could simply ask her."

David's blood turns to ice, and he forgets to breathe. When he finally speaks, the breath bursts out of him in a rush. "I'm not talking about that mission, Lisa. I'm referring to her next trip. She departed three weeks ago."

Lisa's mouth drops open and she pushes her wheeled chair as far from the desk as it will go, until her back hits the wall. "But, sir," she whispers. "That trip never happened."

"What?" David grunts through clenched teeth. His eyes fly back and forth between Lisa and Doug. Doug nods in support of Lisa.

Lisa stands up, her spine stiff and straight. "That mission never happened, sir," she repeats. "Because you aborted it."

———————

David grits his teeth and glares at his sleeping wife on the bed, her wrists still zip-tied above her head. "Wake up," he snaps.

Sarah tries to roll onto her side, her face clouded with sleep and confusion. When she feels the pull of the zip tie on her wrists, her eyes fly all the way open and snap with fury. "David, release me this instant."

He ignores her demand and speaks in a cold, furious tone. "Three weeks ago, you came into my office and interrupted Rosie and I while we were in the middle of a planning session. I sent her on the mission we'd outlined anyway, but just before she was set to launch, her mission was aborted by a comm that came directly from the private line in these quarters. And the only person who could have originated a comm from our quarters was you, Sarah. Which is how you became involved enough to know Rosie was missing in the first place."

David leans over her so that they're almost nose to nose. "Now, you're going to tell me who instructed you to abort the mission, why you were given that directive, and where my daughter is now. Cooperate, and I'll go easier on you."

Sarah narrows her eyes, draws in a breath, and spits in his face.

David jerks back, murder in his eyes.

Sarah laughs. "I'm not going to spend the rest of my life on a barge, picking through flotsam, losing my hair in clumps. You're not going to do anything to me because I'm the first fertile woman in fifty years. You need me much more than I need you." She bats her eyelashes at him. "I'll never forgive you for treating me like this, David. So now I'm going to make *you* suffer far more. I didn't send a comm from our quarters. While you rushed off to answer your precious Achtung, I followed Rosie downstairs and I waited for her on twenty-five. I knew she had to come upstairs sometime, and it didn't take long. She's so gullible! She believed me when I told her you were waiting for her on the roof. I pushed your little bitch daughter down the straws, David. She's not lost, darling. She's dead."

# CHAPTER NINETEEN

July 2, 2018

"What the hell did you do that for?" Carlos yells when we're blocks away and we finally stop running.

"I got scared," I gasp.

"So you scribbled all over a mural?"

"I didn't scribble all over it."

"Semantics." Carlos throws his hands up. "There are, like, three bathrooms downtown that we can use without getting hassled. Now we're down to two. I can't believe you did that, Lita."

I feel like I've been punched in the gut. "I thought you said that wasn't my name."

"I don't know who you are anymore!" Carlos hollers. "What were you thinking? God!"

My face crumples. "I'm sorry."

Carlos breathes rapidly in and out of his nose, his hands on his hips, then balls his fists at his sides. Hearing him call me "Lita" scares me almost as much as...I remember the scene in the coffee shop up on the fortieth floor and I shudder and wrap my arms around my upper body protectively. Why did I ask what year it was? Now I know that it's 2018. And I'm not sure why, but I know that's really, really bad. But that wasn't what kickstarted my fear in the first place. The guy in the green apron. What had he said? I shake my head. I can't remember. I must have blocked it out.

I unwrap my hands from my body and hold them out in supplication. "I don't remember what got me so scared, but the coffee guy said something, and then I asked him what year it was, and he said it's 2018 and that's terrifying and I don't know why. So I grabbed his black marking pen and I ran over to the mural, and I wrote...I wrote..." My voice chokes up and I can't go on.

Carlos crosses the short distance between us and takes my hands, all signs of irritation gone. "Wrote what, Boo?"

I heave a huge, internal sigh of relief that Carlos has switched back to 'Boo,' but I still can't meet his eyes. I stare at the ground and mumble. "Help me Daddy."

Carlos sniffs then, an unexpected sound, and I dare to look up at him. "I...I miss my dad too," he says. "More than I like to think about."

He laces his fingers in mine and he leads me slowly uphill. After a couple of blocks, I risk an apology. "I'm really, really sorry that I ruined your no-hassle bathroom."

"Well," Carlos says, letting our arms swing slowly, "there are still two more. Don't screw those up, please."

"I swear. I won't mess up again."

Carlos squeezes my hand. "Sometimes it just can't be helped. But thanks. I appreciate the effort."

"Hey, you there!"

Carlos and I both snap our heads in the direction of the harsh voice, but it's not about us this time. A man is standing under a fire escape, banging a broom handle against the bottom rung of the access ladder.

"Ah jeez, Ol' Dirty P." Carlos sighs. "He loves those fire escapes."

"Get down from there," the man with the broom yells. "Before I make you come down."

"Do you need to help your friend?" I ask.

"Nah, ODP's got this," Carlos replies.

Up on the fire escape, the tattered man snatches his arm out and grasps the broom handle. He yanks on it and it flies up. Plucking it out of the air, he spins it around in his hand like a fighting stick, aims it, and sends it torpedoing back at the man on the ground, striking him in the center of his chest.

The man staggers backward.

ODP looks right at us, and I wave. "See ya later!" I call out. ODP scrambles higher. In seconds, he's on the third floor, where he throws his leg over the sill of an open window and disappears inside the building.

"See? He's fine," Carlos says drily. "But we still need to get you out of that red dress. Everyone in Seattle must be looking for you in that getup. You're way too easy to spot right now."

"I get to keep the dress, though, right?" I ask anxiously.

"Yeah, of course. But it needs to stay put away for the foreseeable future. Let's go to Goodwill."

---

Carlos's friend Kevin is at work, and he's fine with letting us pick through the new arrivals again. I find a pair of well-fitting but non-descript black jeans and a gray T-shirt with a large darker gray semi-colon printed on the front. By the time we leave Goodwill, it's early afternoon.

"Let's go to the Rainier Valley," Carlos says. "I think it might be best to avoid downtown for the time being."

I nod. I like the sound of 'Rainier' though I don't know why.

Truthfully, as long as I'm with Carlos, I don't really care where we go or what the place is named. I was so scared he was going to leave me when he called me 'Lita' after the incident downtown, but he's been holding my hand everywhere we walk all afternoon and the warm pressure of his fingers in mine has rebuilt my sense of security block by block.

This part of the city is flat, and I quickly become used to it. I like not feeling that fleeting sensation of fear that I always have whenever we head downhill or get close to the water. Things feel like they could maybe even be normal here. We pass by an Oh Boy Oberto outlet store that smells like heaven.

I ask Carlos what they sell.

"Meat," he replies.

We pass about fifteen stores that smell like chemicals and seem to offer the same thing. "What's a nail salon?"

Carlos rubs my fingertips with his thumb. "They take care of your fingernails."

I pull my hand out of his and stare at my short, broken nails. "That's it? That's all they do?"

"Well, toenails too, if you want them to."

I shake my head. "Just when I think I'm starting to figure things out, you throw me a curveball."

Carlos smiles. "Hey, you know what a curveball is."

"Yeah, I like baseball." My eyes widen. "Hey! I like baseball! And football too. I listen to it all the time."

"Like, on the radio?"

I shake my head slowly, uncertain. "I'm not sure."

"It's baseball season right now. The Ms are on the road, but as soon as they're back in town, I'll take you to Sodo, where the stadiums are. Lots of tourists and out-of-towners on game days, makes for great panhandling. You can listen to the game on loud-speakers and hear the roar of the crowd from right outside."

I grin. "That sounds really fun."

Carlos's stomach rumbles so loud that he jumps and I laugh at him. He grins sheepishly. "Ready for lunch?"

"You definitely are," I reply with a smile.

"Dumpsters in this part of town probably aren't even locked," he says. "How about Mexican?"

I nod. I know that word, so I bet that means I like it. We walk a couple more blocks until we come to a storefront with a yellow and red sign reading, "Casa Cosita Authentic Mexican Food."

"Hmm," Carlos muses. "It might not bode well that they feel the need to defend the authenticity of their food in their sign. Want to keep looking?"

"No," I say. "You're hungry. Let's see what they've left for us in the trashcan."

It's located in what Carlos calls a "strip mall," where five or six businesses are all connected together, so we have to walk all the way down to the end of the block before we can double back to find the trashcans at the rear of the store. Carlos is right, they're not locked, and we pull out bags filled with a mushy amalgamation of foods that all have a similar spicy scent. I don't see any plastic spoons or forks, so I scoop up a handful of cheesy rice and I'm just about to put it into my mouth when Carlos lifts a tin can from the trash and holds it up triumphantly.

"Aha! Authentic Mexican food, my ass," he crows. "Rosarita refried beans."

My right hand opens and the rice spills to the ground. I clutch my left temple with my other hand as I'm hit with a staggering headache. I lurch to the side, bounce off the brick outer wall of the restaurant, and crumple to a seated position. I grab my head with both hands now and try to keep my skull from exploding into a million shards of bone.

*Rosarita, Rosarita, my little refried bean.* I hear Daddy's voice in my head, and I see him in my mind's eye. David Columbia, my father. He's holding his arms out to me and I'm rushing into a hug. Behind him, beyond his office window, the sky is yellow-gray-green and I remember everything.

"Boo! Boo!" Carlos is crouched in front of me, cupping my face in his hands. "What's the matter? What happened?"

"Carlos," I rasp. "Oh my god, Carlos. I remember. I remember it all. I know why I'm here. I'm not supposed to be here. Oh my god."

I pull myself to my feet as rapidly as I can on my unsteady legs. The excruciating hammering in my head from wave after wave of unlocked memories seems endless, and now it's joined by nausea and dread. I know why I'm scared. It's 2018, and with one little empty can of refried beans, I remember all of the things that haven't happened yet.

I grip Carlos's hands urgently and search his face. It's full of nothing but concern for me, his friend...his Boo. He doesn't know. He doesn't know he's already dead. A flame of fierce protectiveness flares in the center of my chest, so hot it startles me. I can't leave him. I won't leave him. I squeeze his hands even harder. "Carlos. I got my memory back, and it's not good, but I promise I'll help you."

Carlos knits his eyebrows together. "Help me? What are you talking about, Boo?"

I'm not going to let fear and despair overwhelm me. I can handle this. I'll go back, I'll get more chemicals and bring them with me, right back to this exact moment. I'll find him and bring him home with me. I slap at my vest pocket. I close my eyes and breathe hard through my nose. My vest is gone. My port was removed. *My return chemicals.* I gasp. It was my return chemicals that brought me here in the first place.

I'm stranded. I can't help Carlos. But David Columbia can. My father will help me. And when I tell him about Carlos, he'll understand, and he'll let me help him too – I know he will.

"Carlos. Where's Smith Tower?"

Carlos cocks his head and points behind me. "It's that way,

back downtown. But why? What has that got to do with anything?"

There's no time to waste. I grab his hand and tug him in the direction of the city's skyscrapers. "We need to go there right now. I have to get a message to my dad."

# CHAPTER TWENTY

July 2, 2018

Carlos asks questions all the way to Smith Tower. I can tell he's getting more and more frustrated by my refusal to answer, but how can I explain anything to him? He'd never believe me.

Carlos is a zed. But he's so much more than that. Before, when I'd traveled, I viewed the world in gray-scale. The only splash of color in my mind's eye had been big red Xs over the people. Deleted. Deleted. Dead, dead, dead.

But not Carlos. I've held his hand. He's snuggled me to sleep. He's protected me, again and again, when I couldn't protect myself. My breath catches in my throat. How many times has he saved me from the police when I didn't remember anything about the world I was in? At least three, probably more. If I'd been put in juvie in 2018 with no return chemicals and no way to contact my father.... I shudder at the thought. What if I'd still been in custody during The Collapse? What then?

2018 is cutting it close, but I've calmed down a little bit now. I know I'm going to be okay. And Carlos will be too. Saving Carlos won't cause a conundrum because he's already saved me. That's logical, right?

"Boo?" Carlos's voice has an edge to it. I'm so lost in thought, I have no idea how many times he's tried to get my attention, but I'm certain it's more than once.

"Carlos, I'm sorry. We have to hurry. There is literally no time to waste, we're getting closer to disaster with every minute that passes. I'll try to explain it to you later, but it's going to be hard. I don't think you'll believe me."

Carlos halts. "You're talking crazy. How can you not trust me? After everything we've been through?"

I grind my teeth in irritation at the delay. "It's not that, Carlos," I say through gritted teeth, trying to relax my jaw. "I do trust you. It's just..." I sigh, exasperated. "You wouldn't understand."

Carlos's mouth settles into a firm, thin line. "Smith Tower. Two blocks north, straight ahead." He gestures to a white building with a pointy roof. It's tall enough for a bit of it to survive to my present day, but it's dwarfed by the bigger buildings around it. It must be so hard for Dad to get in and out of it. But that's why he chose the location. For its difficulty. That's where I'll send him the Achtung.

"I need to get to the top floor, north wall."

The lockbox I'll put the note to Dad in is concealed in a false panel at the base of the north wall on the uppermost floor. Dad had me memorize the procedure before I began traveling. Remove the panel, check the weight on the scale. Remove the lockbox, leave my communication and replace the box on the scale. If the weight doesn't change measurably, throw something heavy inside. It doesn't need to be much. Fifty-six years from now, Dad will get an Achtung the moment the weight on the scale changes in our time. I don't know how it works, because it doesn't really make sense to me, but I can remember at least four different Achtungs my dad has had to chase down. It should have occurred to me that there were other time travelers sending messages, since I never had myself.

I shake my head, trying to clear my thoughts. "Do you have paper and a pencil?" I pause and second-guess myself. Will pencil be legible in sixty years, or will it fade over time? "Wait – no, I need a pen."

Carlos is still super irritated with me. "Do I look like the kind of guy who carries paper and a pen in his backpack?"

I don't even stop to think about it. "Yes."

"What happened to you? If I'd known Mexican food would make you so touchy, I would have suggested Chinese."

My laughter catches me by surprise, and it loosens the tight, lumpy feeling in my throat. Things are going to be okay. Yeah, 2018 is close, but depending on what month it is right now, I could have a year before disaster strikes. Maybe even more.

I throw my arms around Carlos and squeeze him in a giant hug. I lean back, my hands still clasped around his waist, so I can look him straight in the eye. "I'm so, so glad and thankful for you, Carlos, you have no idea. I'm sorry I can't explain right now. I promise to try – right after I take care of this business. But it's probably something that you're going to think is really weird, and I need you to roll with it. Will you do that for me? Please?"

Carlos smiles and looks down at me. He's at least a foot taller than I am. "I actually do have paper and a pen in my backpack," he says.

I smile back. "Follow me."

We ride the elevator to the top floor and I'm no longer scared of it. We don't have elevators in my time – they're death traps. They've long since been removed or rotted away. But here, they're very useful. *The shafts in my time can be death traps too.* My eyes narrow and my heartbeat speeds up. Sarah's pretty face, twisted with malice, swims into my mind as I picture her stomping on my fingertips and trying to murder me in the straws.

The door dings and we step out of the elevator. I don't have time to dwell on Sarah right now. I hurry directly to the false panel, dig my nails into the crack in the wood and pry it outward.

"Oh, god, it's another mural inci – " Carlos cuts himself off as I pull out the lockbox. "What the? What is that thing inside the wall?"

"A scale."

"And what did you take out of there?"

"A lockbox." I spin the numbers on the dial until they read 3351. The box springs open.

"How did you know that would be inside the wall?"

I ignore his question and hold out my hand. "Can I have the paper and pen?"

Carlos digs into his backpack and pulls out a spiral notepad and a pen with a white shaft and a black cap. "Look away for a minute please." I don't want him to watch what I write. I'm going to try to explain this to him, but I still don't know how. If he reads my note to my dad, it's just going to raise a million questions that I won't have answers for.

"Boo…"

I grip the pen. "Please."

Carlos sighs and turns around, and I scribble madly.

*Dad. I'm in 2018.*

I chew my lips. Dang it. "What day is it?" I ask Carlos.

Carlos drawls out his answer. "Monday."

"No, I mean the month and the day."

Carlos sighs. "July second."

I go back to my writing. *It's July 2nd. Sarah pushed me into the straws. I didn't die because I used my return chemicals from the aborted trip to escape. I only just got my memories back. Please come get me. Bring three syringes of return chemicals. One for you, one for me, and one for my friend. Meet me on the twentieth floor landing of the south stairwell of Columbia Tower on July 2nd at 9:00 P.M.*

I pause, close my eyes, and take a deep breath. I just defaced the mural on forty this morning. Do I dare risk going into Columbia again so soon? Will Carlos agree to come with me? If he decides I'm crazy and refuses, we won't need that third set of chemicals. Maybe I should give it more time? I do a quick calculation. July 2nd, 2018 to April 19th, 2019. I have two hundred and ninety-one days. More than I thought, in my initial panic. Should I spare a couple days before I meet Dad, to give myself some time to convince Carlos?

I glance up at his stiff spine, his head held high, and I decide not to change the date. More time would probably just serve to drive a wedge further between us. Carlos is never going to be able to wrap his mind around what I have to tell him. A couple more days is just more time for Carlos to convince himself that I'm crazy and leave me.

I lick my lips and turn back to my writing. *I love you*, I write. I underline the last line three times, rip the page out of the spiral notebook, fold it in half, and throw it and the black pen into the lockbox. Carlos turns around at the noise.

"Done?" he says.

"Yeah. I had to keep the pen."

Carlos rolls his eyes. "That's the least of my worries."

I put the lockbox on the scale and replace the false panel, tapping it gently into place with the pads of my fingers.

I rise and take Carlos's hand.

"I can't believe you just did all that without getting caught."

No sooner are the words out of his mouth than the elevator bell dings and the doors slide open. A tall, grimy man steps out and spears us with blazing brown eyes under craggy white eyebrows. Carlos lets go of my hand and throws his hands in the air in exasperation. "Old Dirty! You have got to stop following me around, man!"

I feel like my eyes are going to pop out of my head as I goggle at the man standing before us on the top floor of Smith Tower. "General Safeco?" I say incredulously.

Safeco's eyes glaze over for an instant, his mouth drops open, and he shakes his head violently. He reaches with his right hand and slaps at his left breast, sliding his hand inside his filthy tattered clothing, searching frantically. His hand emerges with a syringe.

"Wait!" I yell. I run toward him, but I see his posture has changed. His training has kicked in. He's on autopilot, and too fast for me.

He mouths the words as he performs the actions with lightning speed. *Plunge. Withdraw. Drop. Slap. Zip.*

I reach him just as he dematerializes, my fingertips grasping at nothing in the space he occupied a millisecond ago. The spent hypodermic needle clatters lightly on the tile floor.

I fall to my knees, grab it, and squeeze it desperately. There's nothing left. Not one drop.

Carlos's voice breaks the unearthly silence. "What the *hell* just happened?"

My crazed, mixed-up brain can't decide whether to laugh or cry, so I do a little bit of both. Maybe it won't be so hard to get Carlos to believe my story after all.

# CHAPTER TWENTY-ONE

June 9, 2074

General Enrique Safeco paces his office, feverishly balling then unclenching his fists. Rosarita Columbia had been right there. Right in front of him. And he'd done nothing.

Safeco rakes his hands through his hair. It wasn't his fault. He'd been a soldier most of his life. His training was thorough and absolute. When it had kicked in, he'd done what he was supposed to do.

He wasn't lying to himself. But still. He'd come face to face with her in 2018 on the top floor of Smith Tower, and he'd plunged his chemicals into his port like the robot he was.

He shakes his head. No. He is no robot. This isn't over.

At a light tap on his office door, he rearranges his features into an emotionless mask. "Come in," he calls somberly.

Ellen enters and snaps a salute.

"At ease."

Ellen relaxes into parade rest, her legs shoulder-width apart, her hands held behind her in formation at the base of her spine.

Safeco scrutinizes her face. Is she the right choice? What other options does he have? He searches her features for several minutes, the silence in the room deafening.

"Permission to speak, sir?" she finally asks.

"Permission granted."

Ellen doesn't try to meet his eyes. She stares straight ahead, her body as still as a statue. "My last climb was a week ago. It was hard, but I passed. I'm hoping to be a welder, sir. I'll need both my arms, and it's also important that I can communicate verbally. I'm honored to be selected to help my people, and if I may, I'd like to request that it be my left leg."

Safeco's brow wrinkles in confusion. He'd been following her up to that last part, but what she said makes no sense. He was sixty-seven years old when he embarked on his last trip. How old did that make him? Seventy-one? Or was he seventy-five now? Had he aged these years too? He doesn't know anymore. This is uncharted territory. He knows people already think he's ancient. He knows they respect him, but he can't give them any reason to question his sanity, and he's not sure how to respond to her last statement, so he sidesteps it.

"That's not why I called you here today, Ms. Banks."

"It's not?"

"No."

The girl's body seems to relax a fraction of an inch.

"Thank you for coming so quickly," he says.

"It was an order, sir."

He likes her spunk. "You're right. It wasn't really a request, was it?"

"No, sir."

Safeco walks to his Gila-shielded window and stands, looking over the city, his hands clasped behind his back. He stays that way for a full minute before he exhales deeply and turns around.

"You're from The Banks."

"Yes, sir. Wells Fargo." She lowers her eyes. It isn't an address to be proud of.

"You've done well in your studies."

She looks up. "I have. I didn't know you followed that kind of thing here in Safeco Tower."

"I have a job that I need assistance with, and my research has convinced me that you meet the criteria for the position."

Her breath catches noticeably. "A job, sir? Working for you?"

Safeco nods. "Yes. But it's not a position you'd be familiar with." He paces back and forth in front of the window. "It is, however, a job utterly critical to the survival of our society."

She blinks solemnly and waits for him to continue.

Safeco likes that she doesn't immediately pepper him with questions. "If you succeed in this mission, your position in The Towers will be secured for life. You'll move out of The Banks into my tower, and I will train you and designate you to be my successor."

She gasps. "Sir! I'm only sixteen. I haven't even passed my final climb."

"I'm serious, Ms. Banks. Few in our world will ever know or understand the debt of gratitude and service we'll owe you after you complete your mission. But I will. And I intend to reward you commensurately."

"Whatever it is, sir, I'll do it for our people, whether I leave The Banks or not."

Safeco stares at her for a long moment, then nods. "I believe you."

She holds her palms out receptively in front of her body. "What is the mission?"

Safeco takes a deep breath. It has to be done. He knows he's ready to reveal the secret for the first time in his life, but he's surprised by how reluctant his mouth is to form the words. He forces it out. "For the last several years, our society has been aided by a small group of special soldiers who perform critical missions. These missions occur…in the past."

The girl's eyes go wide. "The past? Time travel, sir?"

Safeco nods curtly. "Yes."

His eyes fly around the walls of his office. Nothing has changed, and his head feels fine. He exhales a sigh of relief. "It appears you can be trusted. I'm glad for that." Safeco looks out over the flooded city again before turning back to her. "This mission is of such sensitivity that I need you to travel immediately. You will not return to The Banks. You will travel right now, from my tower. Do you understand?"

She nods. "Yes. I'm honored, sir. I won't let you or our people down."

Safeco cracks his first smile of the interview. "Good. The most important thing you need to know about time travel is that we do not speak of it. We must do everything we can to prevent a conundrum. There are rules, laws of time travel, that we've discovered. The first is that you will not be missed, even by people who know you well. Only other time travelers can notice that you're gone. Another important rule is that you can travel through time, but not space. You will depart from my tower and arrive in my tower. Because of this, I'll be giving you an extra year in the past to complete your mission, but we'll get to that. Finally, you cannot confront yourself in the past. If that were possible, I'd be performing this mission myself. You will undoubtedly catch sight of me while on your mission. You must not approach me. Do you understand?"

She nods emphatically. "Yes, sir."

He looks her straight in the eye. "You cannot travel under the name 'Ellen Banks.' We can't run the risk of you becoming part of the historical record under your own name. For this mission, you'll go by the name 'Lita.'"

He scrutinizes her face for a reaction. It remains receptive, with no flicker of recognition. The name means nothing to her. Safeco feels a burst of energy. She's passed the final test.

He ticks two fingers in the air. "Now, the details. Your mission it two-pronged, which you must achieve in the exact order in which I list them. Upon your arrival in July 2017, you are to assimilate into society in whatever way possible. Learn as much as you can about the city and how to move through it without being apprehended. Pay special attention to Smith Tower. Know it inside and out."

Ellen's eyes shoot to the southwest wall of the room, beyond which the pointy tip of Smith Tower pokes out of the floodwaters. She nods firmly. Safeco can tell she doesn't understand the meaning of the task or why it's important, but he knows it doesn't matter. It's her directive, and she'll do it without question.

Safeco folds a finger down. "Your mission objective occurs on July 2nd, 2018. On that date, you must be inside Smith Tower, hiding on the top floor, near the north wall. At some point between daybreak and twilight on that date, a person will enter the upstairs hallway, access a box hidden inside the wall, and leave something inside it. After that person and her companion are gone, your mission is to destroy the box and everything inside."

She nods again. "I can do that."

Safeco folds down the final finger. "Your second objective is to kill the person who accessed the box."

Ellen's brow wrinkles and her eyes cloud, but she shakes it off quickly. "But, sir, if I have to wait until she's gone to destroy the box, how will I know how to find her again?"

Safeco stares into infinity. He can't have Ellen kill Rosarita when she arrives at Smith Tower, or she won't be able to shout "General Safeco" at him to jog his memory and send him home to 2074. But she must see Rosarita, in order to know who the target is. It's the only way to right the course of history.

Safeco finally blinks and speaks in a low, flat tone. "You'll know when it's time. She is not who you think she is."

Ellen presses her mouth into a firm line. "I understand, sir. I'm ready."

# CHAPTER TWENTY-TWO

July 2, 2018

"What just happened?" Carlos stares in wide-eyed shock at the end of the hallway.

I grab Carlos's arm and try to get him to move with me toward the elevator, but his feet are planted to the floor like he's grown roots. "I'll tell you, Carlos, but we need to get in position first. I've sent for help. We need to be there when my dad arrives."

It's like Carlos doesn't even hear me. His feet unfreeze from the floor and he stumbles forward. He drops to his hands and knees and rubs at the carpet where until moments ago, ODP – General Safeco – had been standing. "Old Dirty Plastered," Carlos says wonderingly. "He just vanished, Boo. Into thin air. He was there, he walked out of the elevator, and then..." Carlos flails his hands in the air above his head. "Gone! I swear. He was right here."

I fall to my knees too. I take his hands. "He was there. You're not crazy. I know him, and his name's not ODP. His name is General Safeco, and he's a very important man where I come from. A great man. He's my father's most trusted lieutenant. If my dad had friends, he would be his best one."

Carlos meets my gaze, confusion written all over his face, and I forge on. "I was worried about how I was going to explain it to you, Carlos. I didn't know how to make you believe me." I fall silent as the weight of everything I have to tell him crushes me.

After a moment, Carlos's voice snaps me back to reality. "Where did you go just now, Boo? You're here, but you're not here. You're not going to vanish all of a sudden like ODP, are you?" He chuffs a wobbly laugh, but I know it's a legitimate question.

I shake my head and rise, gently pulling him to his feet. He stands a foot taller than me, and I tilt my face back. We only have a few hours to get to Columbia Tower to meet my father and escape from this world. "No. I'm not going to vanish like that." *Yet. But when I do, you're coming with me.* I guide him toward the elevator. I have so much to tell him.

*Rosie has regained her memories...but at what cost? Her budding relationship with Carlos is put to the test as Rosie struggles to get them both safely to 2074, while being stalked by an unseen assassin. What happens next? Find out in Paradox Rising, Book Two in The Collapse series.*

**Turn the page for a preview!**

PENELOPE WRIGHT

# PARADOX

THE COLLAPSE —— BOOK TWO

# RISING

# SNEAK PEEK AT PARADOX RISING

July 2, 2018 – Rosie

"What just happened?" Carlos stares in wide-eyed shock at the spot where a filthy homeless man just dematerialized in front of him. He pushes his dark brown hair back from his temples and rakes his hands down the sides of his angular face.

"I'll tell you, Carlos, but we need to get in position first. I've sent for help. We need to be there when my dad arrives."

It's like Carlos doesn't even hear me. His feet unfreeze from the floor and he stumbles to where the man he'd known for years as Old Dirty Plastered just plunged a hypodermic needle in his chest and disappeared. He's on a return trip back to the year 2074, where he's from. It's where I'm from, too, but Carlos doesn't know that. Yet.

I'm in as much shock as Carlos, maybe more, because I just recognized ODP for who he really is: General Enrique Safeco, my dad's righthand man, and the person in charge of Safeco Tower, the second most important building in The United Towers. General Safeco is one of the only people in our world who remembers The Collapse – because he lived through it. I just saw him dematerialize as an old man, but there's a present-day version of him still here somewhere right now, an unsuspecting teenager. Is that a conundrum? My head swims. I have so much to think about.

That wasn't the first time I'd seen General Safeco here in 2018, but it was the first time it had happened since I'd gotten my own memories back earlier this afternoon. I'd brought Carlos directly to Smith Tower so I could get a message to my dad to help me return to 2074. I'm going to bring Carlos to 2074, too, so he doesn't die in The Collapse, which is less than a year away. *You can't save Carlos. He's dead already*, my mind whispers, but I shove that stupid thought out immediately. I can do anything I want to tweak the future. I'm a time traveler.

Dangerous thoughts swirl through my head. I'm not supposed to change the future. I'm only supposed to be here to get things we need in my time. Things like multivitamins and anti-radiation medicine and toothpaste, and a million more little items I can carry back in a shield sack to ensure the survival of my people.

I'm the daughter of David Columbia, leader of Columbia Tower and president of our society, The United Towers. I was supposed to travel to 2007 to get tetanus boosters and a few other critical items, but Dad's wife, my stepmother, Sarah, lured me into one of the straws, the empty elevator shafts that slice through Columbia Tower, and pushed me in. Trapped under-water and about to drown, I used the return chemicals in my vest pocket, the ones that were supposed to bring me home from 2007, to save myself from a watery grave. I must have lost several drops of the chemicals when I'd plunged, though, because I'd fallen short of my destination, landing in 2018 instead of 2007. And since I hadn't been wearing a helmet, my brain got scrambled on the journey. I've been here for weeks, with no memory of who I was or how I ended up crashing on top of Carlos's tent in the middle of the night, drenched in filthy, radioactive sea water. The answer is clear now that I have my memory back.

You can travel through time, but not space. I'd been underwater in 2074 when I plunged my chemicals, somewhere close to street level and near Columbia Tower. Here in 2018, that turned out to be a few feet above where Carlos lived on the streets of downtown Seattle.

Carlos drops to his hands and knees and rubs at the carpet where until moments ago, ODP – General Safeco – had been standing. "Old Dirty Plastered," Carlos says wonderingly. "He just vanished, Boo. Into thin air. He was there, he walked out of the elevator, and then…" Carlos flails his hands in the air above his head. "Gone! I swear. He was right here."

I cross to where Carlos is and drop to my knees too. I take his hands. "He was there. You're not crazy. I know him, and his name's not ODP. His name is General Safeco, and he's a very important man where I come from. A great man. He's my father's most trusted lieutenant, and if my dad had friends, he would be his best."

Carlos meets my gaze, confusion written all over his face, and I forge on. "I was worried about how I was going to explain it to you, Carlos. I didn't know how to make you believe me."

Carlos knows I got my memory back – I hadn't exactly been discreet about it when the dam broke and everything I'd ever experienced came flooding back into my mind – but I hadn't shared anything with Carlos, despite him peppering me with questions all the way from South Seattle to Smith Tower.

I'd kept my mouth shut because you can't talk about time travel, except with other chrononauts, or your prep team. It's a huge unbreakable rule. Anything you say to a civilian might unfurl a conundrum – a logical impossibility – that could cause the instantaneous destruction of our entire world. As soon as my memories came rushing back, I realized there was nothing I could say to Carlos that wouldn't be fraught with danger. Everything about who I am is based in 2074, where a few thousand people survive, clinging to life on the top floors of the tallest buildings in Seattle, waiting for the Earth to recover from the catastrophic devastation of The Collapse.

For a long time, the only other time traveler I knew was my dad. Then I found out about General Safeco. As far as I know, it's just us three, but if there are any others, it's none of my business.

Carlos has seen things now. He watched General Safeco dematerialize. Does that mean he's been brought into the time traveler fold, even though he's not one himself? I know I'm grasping at straws, but Carlos stood by me all this time when I didn't know who I was. He saved me from the 2018 police more than once. If I'd been arrested and put into juvie, I'd be as good as dead. I'd never be able to get a message to my dad, and that whole area is deep underwater in 2074. Dad showed me once from a helicopter. In keeping me from falling into police custody, Carlos saved my life. So he's affected the future too. It has to be okay to tell him.

And I'm going to have to take the risk because I plan to make him a traveler too. I'm going to take him back with me to 2074. He won't be here for The Collapse. Carlos is a zed right now, but I'm going to make sure he lives. I've already sent a message to my dad, asking him to meet me in Columbia Tower with three sets of return chemicals. I didn't tell him why in my note, but I know he'll trust me and bring them. Tonight, when we see him in the stairwell of the twentieth floor of Columbia Tower, I'll tell Dad the deal. One set of return chemicals for him, one for me, and one for Carlos. Dad will have to let me do it because Carlos will already know about time travel, since I'm going to tell him before we meet my dad. At that point, it will actually be safer and less likely to cause a conundrum if Carlos travels with us and lives the rest of his life in his future, my present day, 2074. Dad will understand and agree. I know he will. He has to.

I'm still gripping Carlos's hands and I realize we've been

staring at each other this whole time, but I've been so lost in thought, I haven't really been seeing him.

"Where did you go just now, Boo? You're here, but you're not here. You're not going to vanish all of a sudden like ODP, are you?" He chuffs a shaky laugh, but I know it's a legitimate question.

I shake my head and rise, gently pulling him to his feet. He stands a foot taller than me, and I tilt my face back to look him in the eye. "No. I'm not going to vanish like that." *I'm going to do it differently. And when I do, you're coming with me.* I guide him toward the elevator. I have so much to tell him.


July 2, 2018 – Ellen

As soon as the elevator doors slide shut to whisk Rosie and Carlos to street level, the silence of the deserted upper floor of Smith Tower is broken by the whisper of a carabiner skimming down a length of rope. An assassin descends thirty feet from the high point of the roof, landing lightly on the floor. It's a teenage girl, lithe and strong, though shorter than average. Ellen wears a bodysuit of mottled brown and yellow. She planned her outfit to blend into the dappled light and the rafters of the ceiling. It worked perfectly. The bow and arrow slung across her back shifts and dips toward the ground, following the contour of her body. Ellen's been here in the past for over a year, waiting for this moment, and she just failed her mission.

Ellen nearly cried out in disbelief when Rosie stepped off the elevator with that teenage boy at her side. *No.* It had to be a coincidence. Rosie wasn't here to access the box. This wasn't the person she was supposed to kill. As she watched them move down the hallway toward the south corner, her thoughts shifted. Maybe it was the teenage boy who would remove the panel and pull out the lockbox that she knew was hidden within the wall. She could kill him no problem.

But Ellen watched with dread and horror as Rosie peeled away from the boy, went directly to the south wall, pried back the false panel, and removed the box. The boy gave her a pen and paper, and she wrote a note, threw it and the pen inside the box, and then resealed it in the wall.

Ellen's heart hammered in her chest, and she reached back for her bow and arrow. She knew what she had to do. But... kill Rosie? Her letter-mate? The person she would die to protect, who would die for her in return?

Then the elevator door opened again, and out stepped General Safeco himself. Ellen froze. She remembered the direct order he had given her before he'd sent her on this time travel mission. *Do not attempt to approach me.* Ellen dangled in the rafters, watching the whole scene unfold. When General Safeco dematerialized in the hallway, she knew she could make her move, but she stayed put, wracking her brain, reaching back more than a year to replay the conversation she'd had with him before he'd sent her here.

What had General Safeco said, exactly? Destroy the box, *then* follow and kill the person who'd accessed it. Safeco had known this would unfold exactly as it had. He hadn't meant for Rosie to die in this upstairs hallway. Her breath whooshed out of her in a relieved sigh. She hadn't failed her mission. She was still only on step one. She didn't have to think about step two yet. She could shove it out of her mind and wrestle with that later.

Now, Ellen moves like a panther to the south wall of the hallway, pries the panel away from the wall, and pulls out the box. She replaces the panel, tucks the box under her arm, returns to the rope, winches herself in with the carabiner, and vanishes back into the rafters.

# ABOUT THE AUTHOR

Penelope Wright spent a quarter of her life on the east coast and the rest in Washington state. She worked her way through college in restaurants, hospitals, factories, and everything in between, finally graduating summa cum laude from the University of Washington after an absurdly long time. She loves both traditions and new experiences, and will try anything once, except skydiving, which is a hard no. She lives north of Seattle with her husband and two amazing daughters.

## ACKNOWLEDGMENTS

I've always been fascinated by time travel and all the possibilities it holds, and I've wanted to write it for a very long time but found myself making one false start after another. I thank my critique group, Jennifer Bardsley, Laura Moe, Sharman Badgett-Young, and Louise Cypress, for their invaluable insights and developmental help. This book literally would not exist without them, and I cannot thank them enough.

I'd also like to thank my editor, Amy McNulty, for her sharp eyes and excellent attention to detail. Time travel is a difficult beast, and any errors, mistakes, or – gulp – conundrums are mine and mine alone. Huge thanks goes to Nicole Conway for her gorgeous cover designs which I loved the moment I saw them. An extra special thank you to Jennifer Bardsley, again, for formatting the inside to be just as beautiful as the outside.

I'd like to thank my friend Lindsey Wright for beta reading and offering extremely helpful feedback. Additionally, I'd like to thank Lindsey and my friends CarrieAnn Brown and Joie Stevens for being utterly awesome.

Finally, I'd like to thank my husband, Travis Wright, and my daughters, Madeline and Annika, for being the most perfect family I could ever hope for. You're all amazing and interesting people and I'm so lucky you're the ones I get to spend most of my time with.

Made in the USA
Middletown, DE
20 October 2020